FIRES IN FLUX SECTOR

A LADY ELIZABETH COZY IN SPACE

DIANA XARISSA

ISBN: 9798310807662

First edition 2025

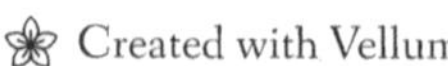
Created with Vellum

AUTHOR'S NOTE

Once again I need to thank my friends from the author community who let me use their names or suggested names for characters in this book.

Please check some (or all) of them out on Amazon. (You might not find them all there - at least not yet!)

Linda Boulanger
Jonathan Brazee
Kelly Collins
Carolyn Dean
Troy Hill
Shawn Inmon
Iris JaKay
Craig Martelle
Tammy Martelle
Honey Phillips
Ava Ross
Michael Ryder

R.L. Syme
Alyn Troy
Jerry Weible

ONE

DAY TWO - FLUX SECTOR

"Fire! Fire! Fire!"

The loud voice woke me out of a sound sleep.

"This is a test of the shipwide fire alert system," the voice said.

I blew out a relieved sigh. "It's just a test," I told Singer, my tiny cat. She snuggled closer to me and shut her eyes tightly.

"This ship is required by intergalactic law to test this fire alert system at least once per sector," the voice said.

"Yeah, but not in the middle of the night," I muttered.

"Please consult the International Galactic Transportation of Intelligent Species Protocol Guide for additional information about this required test."

As the voice stopped speaking, the loud siren blared.

"Fire!"

"We've been through five other sectors," I said to Singer. "I don't remember any fire alert system tests in any other sector."

"Mmmerrooww," Singer said sleepily.

"Section 432034.2004 of the aforementioned guide

contains information relevant to this required test," the voice continued. "Specifically, subsections 34A, 45C, 20.3M, and 209X. We suggest that all passengers aboard the *Lady Elizabeth* consult those subsections regularly."

"Yeah, I'll get right on that," I muttered as I flipped over my pillow.

"Fire! Fire! Fire! This is a test of the shipwide fire alert system. Please remain calm and proceed immediately to your assigned emergency evacuation station."

"What?" I frowned at the ceiling. "If this is just a test, we shouldn't have to evacuate the ship."

A moment later, a different voice came through the cabin's speakers.

"Attention passengers, we are required under intergalactic regulations to test the fire alert system at least once in each sector. Previously, we've met the requirement by testing the system in non-passenger areas of the *Lady Elizabeth*, but we are also required to conduct at least one complete test of the system in passenger areas without providing prior warning. This is that test."

"Great, thanks for that. Can I go back to sleep now?"

"As part of the test, we need the full cooperation of our passengers. The scope of the test is randomized by our onboard computer systems. In this instance, the computer has selected to test our alert system and the subsequent response to the alert. We need to ask everyone to report to their assigned evacuation stations immediately."

"Seriously?" I slid down further under the bedclothes. "No one will miss me if I don't go," I said.

"Fire! Fire! Fire! Please proceed to your assigned evacuation station immediately." The first voice, clearly a mech-bot, was back. "Anyone ignoring this directive will be fined a million credits and removed from the ship when we reach our next planetary excursion point."

"Can they do that?" I asked Singer. "I don't have a million credits. I don't have anything close to a million credits. And I don't want to get thrown off the ship on our next stop. I want to get to Val Segas."

Singer didn't reply.

"Please report to your assigned evacuation station immediately," the voice said again. "We will start scanning cabins for passengers who are not in compliance in two minutes."

I jumped out of bed and changed into the first clothes that I touched. There was no way I was going to start wandering the corridors of the *Lady Elizabeth* in my pajamas. I grabbed Singer and tucked her into my pocket.

"Stay in there and stay quiet," I told her. "I'm not supposed to take you out of the cabin without a leash, and I don't have time to fuss with that right now."

I grabbed the bag by the door. It wasn't as if I'd been planning for an emergency evacuation, exactly, it was just that I liked feeling as if I were prepared for anything. The small bag was filled with emergency food rations for both me and Singer, as well as a few changes of clothes. Those were for me. Singer would be perfectly fine in her thick furry coat. I stepped out into the corridor and looked up and down. I didn't see anyone else.

"Where is everyone?" I muttered as I stepped out of my cabin.

As the door slid shut behind me, another door farther down the corridor opened.

"Do we really have to do this?" a man shouted toward me as he looked out of his cabin.

I shrugged. "I can't afford a million credit fine, so here I am."

He laughed. "I can afford it, but I'd rather not have to pay it. I'd better put some clothes on."

As he disappeared from view, other doors began to open.

"Where are we supposed to go?" a woman asked as she walked out of her cabin. She was wearing oversized pajamas and a pair of fluffy slippers.

"Were we actually assigned evacuation stations?" someone asked.

"I didn't bother going to the safety briefing," someone else said.

"Was there a safety briefing?" a woman asked.

I didn't remember having a safety briefing, but that didn't mean it hadn't happened.

"Attention passengers, we need you all to make your way to the evacuation stations. For those who missed the safety briefing before departure, the evacuation stations are located across from the restaurant on your deck. Please make your way there immediately. Cabins are going to be scanned shortly."

"Finally, some helpful information," a man said as we all walked toward the restaurant.

When we got there, we found a collection of mech-bots hovering near the restaurant's entrance.

"This is a required fire alert system test," one of them said as we approached.

"Yeah, whatever," a man snapped. "We're here. Can we go back to bed now?"

"As part of the test, evacuation times need to be evaluated," the mech-bot replied. "I need each of you to step forward and scan your comms so that we can be certain that every passenger is accounted for."

Nearly everyone rushed forward. I stood back and watched as people pushed and shoved to be among the first to scan. Eventually, as the mech-bot beeped and hummed, people began to move away. I noticed that a short queue had formed with the last few people who needed to scan. I joined the queue as more passengers arrived.

"Once we've scanned, we can go, right?" a man asked.

The mech-bot beeped several times. "We have not been given clearance to release you back to your cabins," it said.

"This is ridiculous," a woman shouted. "It's the middle of the night. I appreciate this is about our safety, but run your stupid test during the day when we're all awake and bored."

The mech-bot beeped again and then seemed to switch off.

"Now what?" someone asked.

"Bot 3904-XDE-94 has malfunctioned," another of the bots said. "Diagnostics suggested an overheated hamstrio circuit. Or it could be an issue with the logicore module. Please continue to wait. The ship's systems are currently evaluating our performance on the required evacuation test."

"I'm going back to bed," an older man said. "And I'll be complaining to Captain Ryder in the morning about this entire mess."

"I'll be complaining to Shawn Inmon," another man said. "Complaining to the guy who owns the ship will get better results than complaining to the ship's captain."

Someone laughed.

"Except Shawn Inmon doesn't own a single thing," another voice said. "He's unlikely to ever own anything, for that matter. His father owns half the galaxy, but he doesn't like Shawn. That's why Shawn got stuck with this assignment. Taking a long-distance spaceship across twenty-six sectors while doing nothing at all is a difficult test for Shawn's abilities. I keep expecting him to accidentally release the croccigators onto B Deck or maybe try to open a vital airlock in an effort to get some fresh air into his cabin."

"The man's an idiot, but he should be able to get the ship excused from fire alert system tests for the next twenty sectors," the first man replied.

"But we really need those tests," someone said. "This ship is supposed to be brand new, but things keep failing all the time. If you ask me, I think this entire fire alert test is just another system malfunction."

A few people muttered their agreement. I slid my hand into my pocket and gave Singer a pat. I could feel her tiny body vibrating as she purred under my touch.

"Good evening," a voice behind the crowd said.

We all turned around. I was surprised to see Colonel Jonathan Brazee standing there.

"You may all return to your cabins now," he said.

"Tell that to the mech-bots," someone shouted.

Jonathan grinned. "They won't be a problem."

A few people began to walk away. The mech-bots hummed and whirred, but none of them said anything. As soon as the rest of the crowd realized that the bots weren't going to stop them, everyone quickly walked away. Jonathan caught my eye as I started to head back toward my cabin.

"Diana, how are you?" he asked.

I shrugged. "I'm okay."

"Have you recovered from everything that happened on Caboluxous?"

"I'm fine," I said. Now was not the time to try to explain

how lost and confused I still felt after everything that had happened on the beach planet we'd visited in our last sector.

"The last I heard, Tara and Jason were both still blaming each other for everything that happened."

"That doesn't surprise me. I'm trying not to hear anything about any of it."

Jonathan frowned. "Tara tried to frame you for her murder. Jason may or may not have been a party to the plan. You should be following what's happening with great interest."

Except I'd thought Jason was my friend. He was the one person in the entire galaxy that I'd thought I could trust. And now that is in doubt, and it's easier to pretend that none of it is happening than to deal with the reality of the situation. I swallowed hard and then shrugged again. "It doesn't matter," I said flatly.

"I won't bother you with the details, then," Jonathan said with a shrug of his own.

He turned and began to walk back down the corridor. I took a few quick steps to match his pace.

"What's going on with the fire alert system?" I asked him.

He grinned at me. "The ship's systems are designed to conduct random fire alert system tests at least once per sector. It recently became apparent that someone had reprogrammed things so that the tests were no longer random. Instead, a single alarm on C Deck was used in each sector to prove that the system was functioning properly. Of course, that test actually proved nothing at all, but it was enough to satisfy the system's requirements under the revised and unauthorized reprogramming."

"Who did the reprogramming?"

"Ah, that's the question, isn't it? No one will admit to

having done it, of course, but there are only a handful of crew members with the necessary security clearance to have made the changes. I'll be keeping an eye on them in the future. Of course, it's also possible that a rogue passenger did a bit of hacking in his or her spare time. There are a small number of passengers on the ship who could have made the changes and gone undetected."

"But it's all fixed now?"

"I believe so. I also think we're going to have a lot more random fire alert system tests over the next sector. The system has never been tested properly under active performance conditions. Now that the dodgy programming has been removed, I would imagine the Safety and Security Protocol will want to test multiple components of the system."

"So we're going to get woken up in the middle of the night again," I said as we reached my cabin door.

"Maybe, or maybe alarms will go off during the day, perhaps while everyone is eating lunch or dinner. The key to proper testing is randomness, of course."

I nodded. "Will we have to report to our evacuation station every time?"

"I doubt it. Most of the tests will probably be tests of the alarms rather than anything else, but you never know. I wouldn't be surprised if the system decided to request actual fire testing, too."

"What does that entail?"

"That depends on what test or tests the system asks for. I've seen everything from asking a member of the crew to strike a match to having the crew start a small kitchen fire deliberately."

"They're going to set the ship on fire?"

"In a controlled manner, to test the ship's fire response systems properly."

I sighed. "Maybe Cenclare wasn't all that bad."

Jonathan chuckled. "Surely you still want to start a new life on Val Segas?"

"I do, but I wish I'd found a different way to get there."

"You can get off the ship at any of our planetary excursion stops."

"Yeah, but then I'd be stuck wherever I'd gotten off. I can't afford to buy myself another ticket to Val Segas. You know I couldn't even afford a ticket on the *Lady Elizabeth*."

"And then Jason was kind enough to buy a ticket for you."

I nodded. "And I'll wonder forever what his motive actually was."

"You're better off wondering than trying to get an answer from him."

I tapped on the panel by the door. It slid open. "Good night," I said to Jonathan.

He smiled. "Good night."

Inside my cabin, I put Singer down and then fell onto the bed still dressed. I was asleep in less than a minute.

MY ALARM WENT off a few hours later. I groaned and then slowly got back to my feet. Since I was already dressed, I decided to leave my shower for after breakfast. In the dining room, it seemed as if everyone was talking about the late-night fire alarm. I sipped extra-dark coffee while I waited for my food to arrive. While I was eating, a member of the crew walked into the room.

"Good morning, everyone," he said loudly. "I'm very

sorry that I'm interrupting your breakfast, but the ship's systems have sent out a request for a very specific fire safety test. Please ignore the alarms while I conduct this test."

I exchanged glances with the woman at the next table. We both made faces as the crew member moved into the center of the room. He pulled an old-fashioned box of matches out of his pocket and lit one. Then he held the match high above his head.

"A fire has been detected in the A Deck restaurant," a mechanical voice said over the ship's loudspeakers. "Everyone should remain where they are and await further instructions."

A moment later, a large mech-bot flew out of the kitchen. It took only seconds to reach the man with the match.

"That should do it," the crew member said, putting his arm down and shaking the match to extinguish the flame.

"Fire!" the mech-bot said loudly. It buzzed and hummed for a second before a panel on the bottom of the bot slid open. Everyone in the room stared as an enormous amount of water dropped out of the bot and onto the man's head.

"I already put the fire out," he shouted at the bot.

"Fire!" the bot replied. An arm lifted and began to shoot white foam at the man. He screamed and tried to run out of the room. The bot followed him, still firing foam at him.

"The fire is out," he shouted repeatedly as he ran in circles.

"The fire is out," the mech-bot said as the stream of foam stopped.

"Yeah," the man said, leaning heavily on an empty chair while he tried to catch his breath.

"The danger is over. The fire is out. I must refill to capacity." The bot flew away.

The man looked around the room. Everyone was staring at him.

"They told me that all I had to do was blow out the match," he said before shaking his head and turning around.

We all watched as he squelched his way to the door. Water dripped from him, and large blobs of foam dropped off with every step. The room remained silent until the door shut behind him. Then we all began to laugh.

I spent the rest of the day studying coding from the course cube I'd been given. Learning to code computer games had long been a dream of mine, and this course was making it a reality. But the work was hard, especially since I couldn't use the inbuilt tutoring system because communication while in deep space was complicated, if not impossible. The course would have been expensive if I'd had to pay for it, though, so I kept working on my own until I understood each section before moving on.

After having had lunch in my room, I went to the restaurant for dinner. I was halfway through my meal when a crew member entered.

"We'll be making an announcement later, but consider this advance warning," he said loudly. "Tomorrow morning at ten o'clock, we will be conducting a more thorough test of our fire management system."

"What does that mean?" a woman shouted.

"It means that we'll be building a small fire in one of the suites on the deck that isn't currently being used," he replied. "It will set off the alarms, but hopefully the fire suppression mech-bots will take care of everything before it becomes a problem."

"What if they don't?" a voice called.

The man chuckled. "The *Lady Elizabeth* is the most advanced and sophisticated ship in InmonCorp's fleet. There are multiple fire-control systems on the ship. You don't need to worry about fire."

"Yeah, I saw the fire-control bot this morning," a man said. "He chased one of your fellow crew members all around the place shooting foam at him, even though the fire was out."

"The bots are programmed to do everything necessary to be absolutely certain that any fire is fully extinguished. The bot was simply doing its job."

"But it can't hold all that much water," another man said. "What happens if the bot runs out of water and foam?"

"There are over a dozen fire-control bots on the ship," the crew member told him. "And they are simply our first line of defense against fire."

"What comes next?" a voice called.

"The bots are the preferred first response because they can dispense water and/or foam in a small and controlled fashion. Every cabin and public area on the ship also has a sprinkler system installed." He pointed to the ceiling above us.

I looked up at the small sprinkler head that was right above me.

"The sprinkler system can spray either water or foam, depending on the nature of the fire," the man said. "The spray covers a much larger area, though. We hope that they will never need to be used because water and foam can cause considerable damage."

"Not as much as fire," someone suggested.

The man nodded. "Which is why the sprinkler system is in place."

"Is that it?" someone asked.

"There is also an active fire-control officer onboard," the man said. "He is responsible for monitoring all fire activity on the ship and responding to alarms as necessary."

"Who is our fire-control officer?" someone asked.

"The role has been filled by different people since we left Cenclare. At the moment, our captain, Michael Ryder, also holds that role."

"As if he doesn't have enough to do," a voice muttered.

"So if the bots run out of foam and the sprinklers stop working, we have to rely on an overworked man dropping everything he's doing and running to the scene. I don't feel safe with that," a woman said.

"There are other emergency measures in place," the crew member said.

"Such as?" someone asked.

"In the case of fires within cabins or other smaller rooms, we also have the capacity to switch off the oxygen supply in the space. That very quickly starves the fire of necessary fuel and extinguishes it," the man replied.

"And too bad if you're in that cabin when the oxygen gets shut off," someone said.

The man smiled. "There are fail-safes in place to ensure that the room is scanned for life forms before such drastic measures are taken."

"I don't know," a man said. "It seems to me that it wouldn't be all that difficult to override those fail-safes. It might be the perfect way to murder someone."

I flushed as every person in the room turned to look at me.

TWO

"Just because I've found a few bodies, doesn't mean I know anything about murder," I muttered under my breath.

"As I said, the test is going to be carried out in an unused space," the man said.

"C Deck," someone said. "Where you're keeping all the murderers who've been caught since we left Cenclare. Maybe this is just a plot to kill them all so you don't have to keep feeding them."

The man looked shocked. "There are a few people staying on C Deck, men and women who have been accused, but not convicted of any crimes. Clearly executing them would be against intergalactic regulations. Our tests will be conducted in an area of the deck far away from the occupied cabins, for obvious safety reasons."

"You're going to set a cabin on fire and hope that the bots can put it out, is that right?" someone asked.

"That is correct. As I said, there are a number of systems in place that will make the test completely safe. We're only notifying passengers because there will be a number of alarms that will sound throughout the testing process."

"Ten o'clock tomorrow?" a man checked.

"Yes, at exactly ten o'clock tomorrow. Just ignore the alarms and other warnings. You will all be perfectly safe here on A Deck."

After finishing dinner and a thick slice of chocolate cake, I made my way back to my cabin. I was giving Singer a cuddle when someone knocked on my door. Singer's excited "meows" told me who to expect before I opened it.

"I wasn't expecting to see you again so soon," I said to Jonathan. I usually only saw him when we were caught up in a murder investigation. Between those, he mostly seemed to keep to himself in his luxury suite on the other side of A Deck.

"Captain Ryder has invited me to come and watch the fire system test tomorrow. I thought maybe you'd like to come along."

"And watch someone start a fire in a cabin on C Deck?"

Jonathan shrugged. "It's something different, anyway. It's always nice to have something different to do. Otherwise, the days can seem very long and very boring."

I thought for a minute. "You're right, of course. Sure. Why not. It might be interesting to see the system at work."

"I'll pick you up here at nine-thirty. Then we can watch them get everything set up before the test at ten."

"Sounds good. See you then."

He nodded and then turned and marched away in the particular gait that retired Space Corps members all seemed to share. I shut my door and then flipped on my screen. I watched a program about a mouse in space that was alternately funny and weird. When it finished, I shut the screen off and got ready for bed.

"Tomorrow, I'm going to go and watch a fire," I told Singer as I slid under the covers. "I'm that desperate for things to do."

She stared at me for a moment before shutting her eyes and seemingly going straight to sleep.

"Yeah, you have the right idea," I said before turning off the lights and doing the same.

THE DINING ROOM was nearly full when I went to breakfast the next morning. There were so few tables available, I wondered if everyone on A Deck was hoping to watch another crew member get soaked and covered in foam or if people were just up earlier today for some reason. I was halfway through my breakfast when the alarm sounded.

"Fire. Fire. Fire. There is a fire in the kitchen on A Deck," the mechanical voice announced. "Please do not panic. Remain calm." The voice got louder and shriller as it continued. "Do not panic. The situation is under control. The fire will be dealt with. Do not panic. Do not panic. Do not pan..."

I frowned as the voice trailed off. *Maybe now would be a good time to panic,* I thought as the door to the kitchen opened and three mech-bots flew out.

"There is a fire in the kitchen," one of them said as all three of them flew around the dining room in a seemingly random fashion.

"Fire!" another shouted. "We're all going to melt. I'm melting now."

I looked at the bot. It looked absolutely fine. I took another bite of my panaffles. The door to the dining room suddenly burst open. Half a dozen fire-control bots flew into the room. They made a complete circuit of the room and then stopped near the door.

"No fire has been detected," one of them said. "We will return to our station."

"The fire is in the kitchen," one of the men sitting near the bots said.

"No fire has been detected," the bot repeated.

"Because you're in the wrong room," the man said. "You need to go into the kitchen."

"No fire has been detected," the bot said again.

The man stood up and walked to the kitchen door. He pulled it open and then waved. "Look in there," he said.

From where I was sitting, I could see smoke in the kitchen. It seemed likely that there actually was a fire in there somewhere. Which was a somewhat worrying thought, actually.

"Everyone should eat quickly," someone said. "If the sprinklers come on, our food will get covered in water and foam."

I grabbed my last slice of bacon off my plate and ate it quickly.

The fire-control bots were still clustered near the door. The other three mech-bots approached them slowly.

"There is a fire in the kitchen," one of them said.

"No fire has been detected," the same fire-control bot replied.

"It's in the kitchen," the mech-bot repeated.

The fire-control bot hummed and buzzed for three seconds. "You can confirm that there is a fire?" he asked the mech-bot.

"There is a fire in the kitchen," the mech-bot said.

"There is a fire," the fire-control bot said. It hummed again and then released its water supply.

The other five fire-control bots immediately did the same thing, drenching the people sitting at the tables under them and leaving a large pool of water on the floor.

The man in the kitchen doorway sighed. "This isn't giving me a lot of confidence in the fire-control system," he said.

"How bad is the fire?" someone asked.

He glanced into the kitchen. "It looks like a pan caught on fire. It's just smoldering now. I think the fire is out."

"The fire is out," one of the fire-control bots said. "We must return to the station to refill to capacity."

As the six bots flew out of the room, the man in the kitchen doorway let the door shut and walked back to his seat.

"If there ever is a real fire, we're all going to die," he said before he sat down.

I finished my breakfast and then walked back to my cabin. Singer was prowling around the space, stalking something that was only visible to her. I gave her a treat and then settled in to tackle the next exercise in my course before Jonathan arrived. I finished just moments before he knocked.

"Ready?" he asked when I opened the door.

I nodded. "Did you hear about what happened in the dining room this morning?" I asked as we walked toward the elevators together.

He sighed. "Everyone on A Deck is talking about it. Luckily, the fire wasn't serious. And it helped the crew identify a problem with the programming that the fire-control bots use."

"What kind of problem?"

"They were using ship schematics for a different ship, so when they flew into the dining room, they thought they were in the kitchen, which is where the fire was reported to be."

"They were using the schematics for a different ship?"

"They were all reassigned to the *Lady Elizabeth* after having previously worked on other ships within the Inmon-Corp fleet. Whoever was supposed to reprogram them for this vessel either forgot to upload the correct schematics or hadn't been provided with them in time to complete their programming before we launched."

"We're all going to die," I said as the elevator finally arrived.

"We're all going to be fine," Jonathan countered. "Today's incident simply proved how vital it is to test the ship's systems on a regular basis. If the required testing had been done properly, that little glitch would have been found before we left Alpha Sector."

When Jonathan pushed the button for C Deck, something buzzed.

"Please scan your comms device to show authorization for that deck," a voice said.

Before Jonathan could do anything, the elevator started to move.

"Do you need to scan or not?" I asked.

He shrugged. "Let's see where we are when the doors open."

A moment later, the doors opened onto C Deck. I shuddered. The last time Jonathan and I had been here, we'd found a dead body. Unlike that day, today there were lights on in the corridor.

"That shouldn't have been allowed," I said.

"They might have overwritten the security protocols for

today. We aren't the only people coming to watch the show."

"Oh?"

"Let's go and see who's here," he suggested.

"Where are the people who are staying on this deck being kept?" I asked as we exited the elevator and turned right.

"In the cabins to the left at the farthest end of the corridor," he told me. "There are about a dozen finished cabins at that end of the hall. The rest of the cabins on this deck are in various stages of completion."

"Have they been working on them while we've been traveling?" I asked.

"I believe there are a few construction bots assigned to continue working down here, but I don't know that they're making much progress. I suppose they might finish another cabin or two during our journey, but the bulk of the rest of the construction will take place once we reach Val Segas."

We reached the end of the corridor and turned the corner. I recognized at least a few of the people standing in the hallway outside one of the cabins. Captain Ryder took a step forward.

"Jonathan, glad you could make it," he said. "We're just getting everything ready."

"Retired Space Corps legend, Colonel Jonathan Brazee, has just arrived," a voice said excitedly. "I'm going to try to get a word with the legend himself before things get properly started."

"Colonel Jonathan Brazee is here," another voice said. "I'm going to try to speak with him."

I took a step back as two women headed toward me and Jonathan.

"Colonel Brazee, can you give me a soundblip?" one of the women said.

"No," the other woman snapped. "Give me a soundblip."

Jonathan shook his head. "No comment," he said.

Both women looked at me. For a moment, I thought one of them might ask me for a blip, but then they both shook their heads and walked away.

"Who are they?" I asked Jonathan.

"Content makers. The sort that make immedieos, those five-minute clips that pretend to be news but are usually just advertisements for things no one actually wants to buy."

I laughed. "I've seen some really good ones, but I didn't recognize either of those women."

"I'm sure they'd both be very disappointed to hear that."

I shrugged. "I don't pay that much attention to makers, just the content. And I watch more long content than immedieos. I really prefer made-up stories more than the sort of stuff you get with immedieos. But what are they doing here?"

"Shawn probably invited them to come and film the fire and the aftermath. He's probably hoping for some good publicity. A lot of the immedieos coming from the *Lady Elizabeth* have been less than complimentary."

"And I've missed them all."

"You haven't missed much. Mostly those two sit in their suites and complain about how boring long-distance space travel is. And then they try to sell enhancers and bath fizzies and the like."

"So who are they? Maybe I've heard of them."

"The tall blonde in the tight white dress is Zarina Seintruber."

I frowned. "Is she related to Carl Seintruber? I've heard of him. He produced some of the most famous long-form content of all time."

"She's Carl's wife."

I looked at the woman again. "I know it's impossible to tell anyone's age, but she looked really young. And I know Carl has to be in his seventies, because he made some of the classics that came out fifty years ago."

"Zarina is twenty-three."

"I see. And the other woman?" I asked, looking at the petite brunette who was wearing a bright red tube dress that matched her lipstick.

"That's Laresta Seintruber. Carl's daughter."

"His daughter? She looks to be about the same age as his wife."

"Laresta is twenty-four. Carl divorced her mother, Natalie, when Laresta was a baby. Natalie left Laresta with Carl and moved to Florzonia. As I understand it, she hasn't seen her daughter in twenty-three years."

"Interesting."

"Carl will be around here somewhere. He produces all of the content for both women."

"They don't seem to get along very well," I said as Laresta pushed Zarina away as they both tried to talk to the ship's captain.

"They're fighting for content. If one of them can get a soundblip that goes titanic, she'll be able to demand even more credits from the advertisers who fund her luxury lifestyle."

I shook my head. "I can't imagine being a content maker."

"Sorry we're late," a voice said. "But we're here."

I looked over at the group of three who were walking

toward us. The man between the two women was the person who had spoken.

"The look on your face suggests that you recognize him," Jonathan said, sounding amused.

"It's Howard Howard," I said in a whisper. The man had long dark hair that was tied back in a low ponytail. He was wearing jeans and a T-shirt that advertised one of his early screen classics. I knew he had to be close to sixty, but he looked a lot younger.

He nodded. "Another well-known producer."

"I love just about everything he produces. The dramas, the comedies, the short vids, everything."

"Zarina used to be in a lot of Howard's content," Jonathan said.

I took another look at the blonde. "She does look vaguely familiar."

"She stopped working with Howard when she married Carl about a year ago."

I shrugged. "I can barely remember what I watched last night, let alone something I watched over a year ago."

He nodded.

"The woman on the left in the flowered dress is Honey Phillips." She was a pretty blonde who looked younger than she probably was.

I gasped. "She writes the series *Unexplored Planets.* I love that series. I've seen every episode at least twice. Every story takes place on a different planet, inhabited by a different alien race." I blushed. "They're mostly romances."

"I know. The woman with her is Ava Ross. She also writes that same sort of thing." Ava looked to be of a similar age, with light brown hair that fell in soft waves around her face.

I shook my head. "She writes *Planets Beyond.* Her

heroes are always outcasts or misfits on their planets. Then they find love and live happily ever after. But it isn't really the same sort of thing."

"If you say so." Jonathan looked amused by my attempt to explain the differences between what the two women wrote.

"But why are they here?" I asked as they leaned against the wall behind us.

"I suspect it's research. Both women write stories set in space, which means scenes on spaceships. It isn't often anyone gets a chance to watch fire-control bots in action, especially not fighting a real fire. They'll both probably record the entire thing and then use what they've seen in future stories."

"Wow. I guess I never thought about how they learn about the stuff they write about."

"I'm sure they both do a lot of research."

"What's he doing here?" I asked as Craig Martelle walked up to join the group waiting in the hallway.

"I can think of a number of reasons why he might be here."

I stared at Jonathan. "Want to give me just one?"

He laughed. "I don't think it matters."

"Who is the woman with him?" I asked as Craig said something to the woman by his side. She was shorter than Craig. Her hair was brown, and she was wearing a headband with a large bow on top, centered between two circles of what looked like gold.

"That's Craig's sister, Tammy," Jonathan told me.

I frowned. "Tammy Martelle? *The* Tammy Martelle?"

He chuckled. "There might be more than one."

"Yeah, but I think only one of them is entitled to wear that headband."

"When you found your own planet, you can wear whatever you want," Jonathan said.

"I never realized that she was Craig's sister. And I didn't know she was on the ship."

"She joined us when we stopped on Caboluxous. She spends a few months each year there, soaking up the sunshine. She probably won't stay with us all the way to Val Segas. But this gives her a chance to spend some time with her brother."

"I've been told she's the most organized woman in the galaxy."

"She took a barely habitable planet and turned it into one of the most successful planets ever. That requires a tremendous number of organizational skills, among other things."

"Who else is here?" I asked, looking around. "We don't have to talk about Shawn or Jerry."

Shawn Inmon's father owned the ship. It made sense that he would be there when some of the systems were being tested. Jerry Weible was his assistant, a man with ice-cold eyes. I found him scary even now, when he was on the other side of the hallway and hadn't appeared to have even noticed me.

"That's Iris JaKay," Jonathan told me, nodding at the tall woman standing near the captain. "She's the ship's Nadoian."

"I didn't know we had a Nadoian."

"We didn't, not before Caboluxous. She joined us there."

Iris had long brown hair that flowed down her back and nearly touched the floor. She was wearing a long dress and as she spoke to the captain, her hands never stopped moving.

"I wish I could understand what her hands were saying," I told Jonathan.

"I learned a bit of Nado over the years. My crews nearly always had at least a few Nadoians on board. It's incredibly complex, though."

Nadoians had a simple spoken and written language that allowed them to communicate with everyone around the galaxy. They also had an incredibly complex language entirely communicated with their hands. I'd been told that they used their hands to express their deepest thoughts and emotions. It was a language that really needed to be learned from infancy in order to truly understand everything that it conveyed.

When I'd been about fourteen, I'd become fascinated by it and had attempted to learn a few basic words, but I'd quickly become overwhelmed by how words changed within different contexts in ways that confused me. The only thing I could remember now was the sign for "help" that was to be used only in the most severe of emergencies. I'd always told myself that it might be useful one day, should I ever find myself with a Nadoian in an emergency.

"They like to send their people everywhere in the galaxy to report back on what is out there," Jonathan said. "They prefer to have things explained to them through their signed language. That means sending out a lot of people who can make those reports."

I nodded. "I was told that there are hundreds of Nadoians traveling around the galaxy and reporting back on what they've found."

"That's correct. And now we have one reporting on life on the *Lady Elizabeth.*"

I watched the woman's hands moving gracefully in

front of her. Each of her fingers seemed to have a job of its own to do as she talked.

"Does Captain Ryder understand Nado?" I asked after a minute.

"I doubt it very much. Most Nadoians can't help themselves from using their hands whenever they talk, even when they know that no one around them can understand what they're saying."

The door to one of the cabins suddenly slid open. A fire-control bot emerged from the cabin.

"We are ready to begin the system test," it said.

THREE

"Becca isn't here," Captain Ryder said.

The bot bobbed up and down a few times. "We are ready to begin," it said again.

"We're just waiting for the Chief Medical Officer," the captain said.

"There is no danger," the bot said. "This is a test of the fire-control system. We do not need a medical officer."

"Standard ship safety protocol requires the ship's Chief Medical Officer to be here," the captain replied.

The bot bobbed a few more times. I turned when I heard footsteps coming down the corridor.

"That will be Becca," the captain said.

Everyone watched the corner. I'm sure a few people looked disappointed when Troy Dyffryn appeared.

"I'm sorry I'm late," he said, giving us an awkward smile.

"I don't believe you're needed here," Captain Ryder said.

"I'm the ship's official photographer. I'm supposed to attend every special event," Troy replied. "And this is the first day I've been allowed out of bed. I need to make up for lost time and take lots of pictures."

"First of all, this isn't a special event. This is a fire-control system test," the captain replied. "And secondly, no one here is going to want to buy pictures of themselves watching a fire-control test. You're supposed to take pictures of guests enjoying their time in space. This isn't the place for pictures."

Troy shrugged. "I overslept and missed breakfast. I thought I might get a few interesting pictures down here. I've never been on C Deck before."

"How did you even get down here?" Jerry demanded. "You weren't on the list."

"I just got on the elevator and pushed the button for C Deck," Troy said.

Jerry shook his head. "I thought you put security in place to make sure that only certain people were able to access C Deck today," he said to the captain.

"My security team was supposed to take care of that," he replied. "I had to use my comms in order to access C Deck today."

"So did I," Shawn said. "I almost forgot how to do it, too."

Jerry frowned. "Who else had to use their comms to get down here?" he asked.

No one moved. Jerry scowled.

"We've been working down here," Howard said.

"And so have we," Zarina said.

Howard frowned. "I was told that we would have exclusive access to certain areas," he said to Shawn. "That is what I paid for."

"We're supposed to have exclusive access to this deck,

too," Zarina said. "Carl paid a fortune for the use of the space for shooting."

Howard looked at Shawn. "I can't believe that you deliberately charged both of us exorbitant sums for the same exclusive access. Surely there must have been some mistake." His tone was mocking, as if he knew for a fact that InmonCorp had tried to cheat both men.

"I believe the original plan was to assign each of you to different sections of the deck," Jerry said. "Things became complicated when we had to unexpectedly accommodate guests on this deck."

"In light of the complications, I assume InmonCorp will be refunding some of the fee that I paid for what is no longer exclusive access," Howard said.

"Yeah, Carl wants some credits back, too," Zarina said.

Laresta laughed. "Usually I'd remind you that you have no business speaking for my father, but when it comes to getting credits back, everyone knows that's what my father would want."

"Where is your father?" Howard asked. "I have a few things I want to discuss with him."

Laresta shrugged. "He's supposed to be here. He probably fell asleep in front of his screen while editing something."

"No doubt one of your immedieos," Zarina said with a fake smile.

Laresta took a step closer to her. "My father will get bored with you before we get to Val Segas. I'm his daughter. I'll be a part of his life forever. You'll be lucky to make it to sector ten, really."

Zarina laughed. "Carl loves me. And he'll be far less enamored of you once we start having our own children." She patted her flat stomach. "Maybe we've already started."

Laresta looked stunned. "He doesn't want any more children. Especially not at his age."

"I can be very persuasive," Zarina said with a smug smile. "Think what pregnancy and a baby will do for my immedieos. So many new advertising markets to tap."

"I'm so sorry," Becca said as she ran around the corner. "I had a small emergency to deal with before I could get here."

"I hope nothing is seriously wrong," Shawn said.

She shook her head. "Linda's dat, Gabby, isn't well."

"You aren't an animal doctor," the captain said.

Becca nodded. "But we also don't have one on the ship. The veterinary mech-bot didn't seem to know what to do, so I took a look at her."

"Is she going to be okay?" I asked. I'd met the small hybrid animal a few sectors ago and found her charming.

"I think she just ate something she shouldn't have. Dats are known for eating anything and everything. Linda tries hard to keep her from getting into things she shouldn't, but Gabby is a smart little thing. She loves finding ways to open cupboard doors and once she's opened them, she's going to eat anything that looks like food," Becca told me.

"Are we ready to proceed?" the bot in the cabin doorway asked.

Captain Ryder looked at Shawn. He looked at Jerry. Jerry nodded.

"We're ready," the captain said.

"You may all enter the cabin," the bot said before it slowly reversed back into the cabin.

We made our way into the cabin's small living space. I was shocked at how tiny it was.

"It meets intergalactic regulations for cabin space allocation for long-distance space travel," Jonathan said in my ear.

I shook my head. My cabin on A Deck often felt claustrophobic. And I was only on A Deck because I'd been given an upgrade after I'd found that body on C Deck. The ticket that Jason had purchased for me had been for B Deck. The one time I'd been in a B Deck cabin, I'd realized how incredibly fortunate I'd been to be upgraded. Now, standing in a room on C Deck, I found myself thinking that the cabins on B Deck weren't as bad as I'd thought.

"Obviously, this cabin is only partially completed," Jerry said from where he was standing near the center of the room. "The bed has been fitted, but none of the storage compartments are in place."

I looked at the bed that was folded up against the wall. When it was brought down, it would almost fill the entire space. "Where will they put the storage compartments?" I whispered to Jonathan.

"Anywhere they can be squeezed in," he replied.

"We're going to start the fire on the table," Captain Ryder said.

He walked to the center of the room and used his foot to push a button on the floor. After a few seconds, a small table began to rise out of the floor. It lifted a few millinches and then stopped. The captain sighed. He tapped the button again. The table very slowly sank back until it was flush with the floor. The captain tapped the button a third time. This time, the table rose at least twice as high. When it stopped, the captain reached down and pulled the table up as far as it would go.

"These cabins are unfinished," Jerry said. "Obviously, little snags like that will be taken care of long before this cabin is made available to guests."

Shawn nodded. "Yeah, of course. Although it seems easy enough to just reach down and pull the table up."

"Except now it's probably stuck in place," Craig said. "Which means if someone was staying in this cabin, he or she wouldn't be able to unfold the bed."

Shawn gave him a confused look. "The bed? Where is the bed?"

"It's here," Captain Ryder said. He put his hand on the flat panel that was the base of the folded-away bed.

"How do you sleep on that?" Shawn asked.

"It comes down from the wall," Jerry told him.

"Neat! Can I see?" Shawn looked as excited as a small child.

Captain Ryder gave him a tight smile. "Perhaps we could arrange for you to tour one of the completed cabins on this deck after the safety test has been successfully completed."

Shawn shrugged. "Sure. I guess. I don't have anything else to do this morning, do I?" he asked Jerry.

Jerry hesitated and then shrugged. "Nothing that can't be rearranged if necessary."

"But first, there's going to be a fire, right?" Shawn asked.

The captain nodded. "I'm going to ignite one of the cushions from the bed," he said, putting a large red square cushion on top of the table.

"Where did that come from?" Shawn asked, looking from the folded-up bed to the table and back again.

"It actually came from a different cabin," the captain told him. "The bed in this cabin is simply a frame. The cushions will be added later, after construction is finished in here."

"Isn't the bot supposed to leave?" Jerry asked.

Captain Ryder sighed. "Yes, of course." He looked at

the fire-control bot. "You need to go back to the station and power down until the alarm sounds."

The bot bobbed twice. "Perhaps it would be better if I remained here as a precaution. Other bots will be dispatched when the alarm sounds, but if anything goes wrong, I'll be here to take care of the fire."

"We need to test the system completely. You shouldn't even know that a test is happening," the captain replied.

"I will go back to the station and erase my memory banks," the bot said. "The alarm will be a surprise to me at that point."

"That's good," Jerry said.

We all watched as the bot slowly left the room. Captain Ryder slowly counted to twenty.

"He should be back at his station by now," he said.

"How long does it take for him to wipe his memory banks?" Craig asked.

Jerry sighed. "We probably need to wait a bit longer," he said.

"The door needs to be shut," Captain Ryder said. "The bot will have the necessary codes to get access. Or it should. That's something we need to test."

Howard was standing closest to the door. He tapped the button next to it to shut it.

As the door slid shut, Troy picked up his camera and started taking pictures. "Don't forget to smile," he said brightly.

"I don't think this is the time for pictures," Captain Ryder said.

"I think it's always time for pictures," Laresta said, striking a pose.

Zarina wasn't about to be outdone. She and Laresta posed for a dozen or more photos while Troy snapped away.

He took a few of Honey and Ava and then turned his camera toward Shawn.

"Okay, that's enough," Jerry said sharply.

Troy turned and focused his camera on the captain, who was still standing next to the table.

"Right, here we go," Captain Ryder said. His flaminizer flicked and ignited. He held the flame to the edge of the cushion. For a moment it seemed as if the cushion wasn't going to ignite, but then I noticed that one corner had started to burn. The captain switched off the flaminizer and put it back into his pocket. Then he stepped away from the cushion.

"We need to stand as far from the door and the cushion as we can," he said.

In such a tiny room, getting away from both objects was almost impossible, especially when there were so many of us crammed into the small space. We all stepped back so that we were pressed against the walls as the cushion continued to burn slowly.

"I thought everything in our cabins was supposed to be fire-resistant," Howard said as we all watched the flames.

"Everything in your cabins is fire-resistant," the captain told him. "If you tried to ignite the cushions on your couch or bed, you wouldn't get this sort of result. I soaked this cushion in a flammable agent especially for this test today."

"Why hasn't the alarm sounded?" Honey asked.

"It should sound momentarily," Jerry said.

I looked at Jonathan and then found myself shuffling slightly closer to the door.

Captain Ryder coughed and then moved farther away from the table. A moment later the alarm began to sound.

"Fire! Fire! Fire! A fire has been detected on C Deck. Please remain where you are and await further instructions," the mechanical voice said. "There is a fire on C Deck. Please avoid C Deck if at all possible."

"Not possible," Jonathan said before coughing.

"It's getting really smoky in here," I said as my eyes started to water.

"The fire-control bots will be here soon," Captain Ryder said.

I blinked several times and then coughed.

"You didn't tell me that I needed to bring emergency oxygen for everyone," Becca said. "We should all be wearing protective masks with supplemental oxygen."

"The bots..." Captain Ryder started.

"This is fire-control," a voice at the door said. "A fire is suspected in this cabin. We will be entering in three, two, one.."

Nothing happened.

"We will be entering in three, two, one..." the voice said again.

The door remained closed.

"We need to get out of here," Becca said, taking a step toward the door.

"Yeah, this isn't safe," Shawn said. "The table is on fire now."

I looked over and saw flames shooting out from the center of the table.

"The mechanism is melting," Jonathan said. "We need to get out of here and those bots need to get in here."

"Open the door," Jerry said.

Howard hit the button. The door opened. Two fire-control bots flew into the room.

"Fire confirmed," one said.

"Electronics are burning. Deploy foam," the second said.

The first bot started shooting foam at the table. For a moment, I thought it was going to be enough, but the force of the foam knocked pieces of burning cushion onto the rug under the table. The fire started to spread at an alarming rate. As the second bot began shooting foam at the table, everyone rushed out of the room.

"There aren't any sprinklers in there," Captain Ryder said as a third bot flew into the cabin.

"The cabin isn't being used. Sprinklers are not necessary," Jerry said.

"Maybe it would have been smarter to start a fire in a room with working sprinklers," Craig said before coughing violently.

Captain Ryder looked at Jerry. "I think the room can be sealed," he said.

Jerry nodded. "That seems like the easiest solution. The bots aren't doing much besides spreading the fire around."

I glanced back into the cabin. Bits of flaming cushion had been scattered everywhere. The rug was burning rapidly.

"Is everyone out of the room?" Captain Ryder asked.

We all looked back into the room. It was a small space without any furniture, so it was obvious that the room was empty. Jerry pulled out his comms and tapped a few times. The three bots emerged from the room.

"Emergency protocol six, three, nine," Captain Ryder said to the bots.

"Scanning," the first bot said. "No life forms detected. Sealing the space."

The door slid shut.

"Sealing error. Nine, three, four," the bot said.

"What is that?" Jerry demanded.

Captain Ryder shrugged. "I don't think the door is

sealing properly. I'm going to try to override the error and see if we can get oxygen shut off to the room anyway."

He typed a command into his comms. One of the bots began to whir and click.

"Oxygen supply has been shut off to cabin C166," it said.

"How long will it take to put out the fire?" Zarina asked.

"If the seal was complete, the fire will go out as soon as it's consumed all of the oxygen in the room. If there is a gap in the seal, then some oxygen might continue to get in. I'm hoping it won't be enough oxygen to keep the fire alive, but only time will tell," the captain replied.

"The bots can detect when the fire is out, can't they?" Howard asked.

"They can scan the room for hot spots that would indicate that the fire was still burning," Jerry said. "We'll have them check momentarily."

"This is so cool," Laresta said. "We nearly burned to death. This is going to go titanic for sure."

"For both of us," Zarina said.

"But for me first," Laresta said. "My father is going to put my immedieo together first."

"Maybe. Or maybe not," Zarina said with a smug grin.

"Where is my father?" Laresta asked. "He said he'd be here."

Zarina shrugged. "He left our suite before I did. He said he'd meet me down here. I don't know where he's gone. I've messaged him a dozen times since I got here, but he hasn't replied."

I felt a rush of fear. When I looked at Jonathan, he had a grave expression on his face.

"I'm sure he's fine," I whispered.

Jonathan nodded. Then he looked at the cabin door in front of us.

"No one was in there," I said.

"Scan for fire inside the cabin," Jerry told one of the bots.

It clicked and whirred. "There are three small fires inside the cabin," he said. "They appear to be shrinking in size and ferocity."

"We need to wait until they're out and then slowly reintroduce oxygen into the cabin," Captain Ryder said. "Then we can see how much damage has been done."

"It's a good thing it wasn't a cabin we were using," Shawn said.

Jerry nodded. "But we never would have done a live test in an occupied guest cabin."

"But we could," Shawn said. "Our fire-control systems are the best in the galaxy."

There was a moment of awkward silence before Ava laughed.

"If that was the best in the galaxy, the galaxy is in trouble," she said.

"I'm a bit concerned about how quickly the rug ignited," Howard said. "It looked exactly like the rug in my cabin."

"We use premium quality, fire-resistant carpeting in every part of the ship," Captain Ryder said.

"That rug caught on fire awfully quickly," Honey said.

"What about now?" Jerry asked the bot.

"There is no sign of fire in cabin C-166," it said.

"Reintroduce oxygen," Captain Ryder said.

"Oxygen flowing," the bot said. "Smoke is being cleared."

"Is the cabin safe?" Jerry asked after a moment.

"Yes," the bot said.

Captain Ryder walked to the door. He tapped on the lock panel with his comms. For a moment, nothing happened, then the door slowly slid back. I smelled smoke and melting electronics. Jerry was the first into the room. The rest of us slowly followed.

The cushion that had started the fire was all but gone, completely incinerated by flames. The table had been burnt down to less than half of its height. I could see charred wires and broken electronic connections in the mangled remains. The rug had been burned away nearly everywhere, revealing the thin layer of the fireproof cladding that lined the ship's walls and floors.

"As you can see, the ship's systems managed to put out the fire," Captain Ryder said. "It didn't go as seamlessly as we might have hoped, but the fire is out, and the ship was never in any danger."

"You need to check your systems," Howard said. "The bots couldn't get into the room. Half the stuff in here appears to be flammable. And the door didn't seal properly."

Captain Ryder nodded. "We will be reviewing everything that happened here today. In the meantime, thank you all for coming."

"What about the bathroom?" Troy asked. "It looks as if the fire went right up to the door. Maybe it got under the door."

He pushed the button to open the door to the adjoining bathroom. Someone screamed. I started to back up, unable to tear my eyes away from what I was seeing. Jonathan grabbed my arm and spun me around. That gave me a clear view of Iris, her face pale, as she desperately signed "help" over and over again.

FOUR

"Everyone needs to calm down," Becca said as she walked toward the body that was sitting on the toilet in the bathroom.

"Calm down? That's my husband," Zarina shouted.

"It's my father," Laresta said.

I frowned. I hadn't recognized the man, but it had been a long time since I'd seen a picture of Carl Seintruber. The man I remembered was young and carefree with thick dark hair and a bright smile. The man in the bathroom was old, bald, and grimacing.

I turned back around and watched as Becca slipped a medical monitor onto the man's wrist. It beeped twice before falling silent.

"He's dead, isn't he?" Zarina demanded.

"I think we need to treat this as a crime scene," Jonathan said.

Captain Ryder looked surprised. "He must have gone into the bathroom and then fallen asleep," he said. "The bots probably didn't scan the bathroom for life forms. He must have died from lack of oxygen."

"I thought each room on the ship sealed individually," Howard said.

"In passenger cabins on B and C Decks the entire cabin is considered a single space," Captain Ryder said.

"But the bots aren't programmed to scan the entire cabin before the cabin is sealed?" Craig demanded.

Captain Ryder shrugged. "I'd have to check their programming."

"Everyone needs to be questioned," Jonathan said. "Security needs to take statements."

Jerry nodded. "I'll arrange it," he said, stepping into the corridor.

"It was just a tragic accident," Captain Ryder said.

"I'm not convinced of that," Jonathan said.

The captain frowned at him. "Not every death is murder," he said.

"Let's let Becca make that determination," Jonathan suggested.

"Becca is going to need some time to reach any determination," Becca said. "Right now, I have no idea what killed the man. His death needs to be treated as suspicious for the time being, though."

"That makes it sound as if you think my father might have been murdered," Laresta said.

"That's one possibility," Becca said.

"Everyone loved my father," Laresta protested.

"Everyone loved Carl," Zarina said. "Except for Howard, of course."

Everyone in the room turned to look at Howard.

He laughed uneasily. "We were business rivals, but outside of the business world, we were friends," he said.

"You were not friends," Zarina said. "Carl hated you and you hated him."

"We had a friendly rivalry. But I had nothing to gain from his death."

"Rumor has it you've been planning a move into immedieos," Craig said.

Howard flushed. "I make art, not pointless clips of nothingness."

"Honey, I was told you were going to write a few immedieos for Howard," Craig said.

Honey shrugged. "I write whatever Howard asks me to write. I can write series that fill hours and hours of screen. Or I can write five-minute scripts that can be shot in less than an hour."

"This is pointless," Howard said. "We don't even know that the man was murdered."

"Everyone needs to be silent." The security bot that flew into the room stopped in the center and hummed aggressively. "I will speak to each of you in turn after I examine the body."

"The body is my problem," Becca told it.

The bot buzzed loudly. "Examination of the body is being deferred to Becca Syme, Chief Medical Officer on the *Lady Elizabeth*. Her full report will be appended when available."

"I don't have time for this," Howard said. "And neither do Ava and Honey."

"A man is dead," Jonathan said, his voice low and serious. "You can make time."

Howard looked as if he wanted to argue, but one look from Jonathan had him clamping his lips together.

"I need a space where I can conduct my interviews," the bot said.

"You can use the cabin next door," Captain Ryder said. "And Colonel Brazee can help you."

The bot started to hum again. "Colonel Jonathan Brazee, retired Space Corps? He is not an authorized criminal investigator on this ship."

"There aren't any authorized criminal investigators on this ship," the captain replied. "Colonel Brazee is the best we have."

"Shawn Inmon is this ship's authorized investigator in case of criminal activity," the bot said.

Captain Ryder sighed. "I don't think..." he began.

"Awesome," Shawn said. "I'll interview everyone. Let's get started."

"I do think that Colonel Brazee..." the captain started to say.

Shawn held up his hand. "I can always bring in the colonel if I need to. For now, I'll conduct the necessary interviews in the cabin next door. I hope it has chairs. We've been standing for a long time."

Shawn, the bot, and Captain Ryder all left the room together. A moment later, the bot returned.

"Remember, no talking," it snapped before heading toward the door. "And you keep your hands quiet," it added to Iris.

She flushed and then looked down at her hands. The bot beeped menacingly several times before flying out of the room.

"I'd have a lot more confidence in the investigation if you were heading it up," Howard said to Jonathan.

He shrugged. "Let's hope the bot is up to the job."

A moment later a familiar face appeared in the doorway. Linda Boulanger was pushing a large medical gurney. She nodded at everyone as she pushed the gurney to the bathroom door.

"Take lots of pictures before you move the body,"

Jonathan said to Becca.

She nodded. "I have video, too, from the time Troy opened the door."

"Excellent," Jonathan replied.

With nothing else to do, we all stood and watched as Becca took a few more photos with her comms device. Troy used his camera to capture several as well. A medical bot arrived as they were finishing. Becca and the bot worked together to get the body onto the gurney.

"There isn't any chance he's still alive, is there?" Zarina asked.

Becca shook her head. "I'm sorry."

Zarina burst into tears as Linda pushed the body out of the room.

"I'll be there as soon as I can," Becca called after her.

I was starting to think about sitting on the floor when the security bot returned. It surveyed the room. Zarina was sobbing in one corner. Laresta was crying on Honey's shoulder. Everyone else was simply standing in place, waiting.

"We will start with the widow," the bot said.

Becca held up a hand. "Can you take me first, please? I'd like to get started on the post-mortem."

"Take her first," Zarina said. "The sooner we can find out what happened to my husband, the better."

"I do have other places to be," Howard said.

"That will be taken into consideration," the bot said. "Let's go," it said to Becca.

As they left the room together, I slowly slid down the wall until I was sitting on the floor. The cladding was cold and hard under me, but that was still better than standing. After a minute, some of the others followed suit, sitting down wherever they happened to be standing. Troy took a few pictures and then put his camera away. He sat down and then leaned against the wall and shut his eyes. A few moments later, he started to snore.

With nothing else to do, I started counting the odd noises that were coming from Troy. He'd made sixteen of them before the door opened again.

"Mrs. Seintruber? We're ready for you now," the bot said.

Zarina stood up and took a few wobbly steps forward. "I can't do this," she said.

"You need to be strong for Carl," Jonathan said. "You need to tell them everything you can that might help them work out what happened to him."

"He fell asleep in the bathroom. That wasn't the first time," she said.

"But it was the last," Laresta snapped.

Zarina shot her a quick look and then followed the security bot out of the room.

The commotion had woken Troy. I waited anxiously for him to fall back to sleep. Instead, he pulled out his comms and began scrolling through it. He was still at it when the bot returned and took Laresta away for questioning.

"I really do have other places to be," Howard said as the door shut behind Laresta.

"We all do," Craig said. "No one wants to be here, waiting to be questioned about someone's death."

"While we wait, we should talk," Howard said. "I'd love a soundblip from you about what happened on Alzaska."

Craig shook his head. "No comment."

"What about you, Tammy? Any comment?"

"I've never been to Alzaska," she said flatly.

"But you're Craig's sister. I'm sure he's told you all about the mission that drove him out of Space Corps," Howard said.

"Craig and I talk about many interesting things," she said.

"Do you talk about how many credits you've embezzled from your little planet on the edge of the Oklamanas system?"

Tammy laughed. "If you're hoping for an angry denial, you're going to be disappointed. I'm not even going to dignify that remark with a comment."

"I love your headband," Honey said.

"Thank you," Tammy replied.

"That's every bit of gold ever found on her planet," Howard said. "Or so I've been told."

Tammy just shook her head.

"We aren't supposed to be talking," Jonathan said in a mild tone.

Howard laughed. "We've nothing else to do."

The door opened and the bot flew back into the room. "Howard Howard Howard Howard Howard," it said.

"Only two of them," Howard said as he got to his feet. "Bots always get confused by my name," he added.

"Please come with me," the bot said.

As they left the room, Tammy looked over at Jonathan.

"Colonel Brazee, hello," she said.

He nodded at her. "Ms. Martelle," he said.

She shook her head. "I'm just Tammy. And that goes for everyone in the galaxy. I don't put much stock in fancy titles."

"Then you should call me Jonathan."

Tammy glanced at her brother before looking back at him. "Titles that have been fought for and won are a different thing."

"Then I should call you Queen Tammy."

She laughed loudly. "I did fight hard for my planet, but

never so that I could be called the queen of anything. And at the end of the day, my life was never at risk. If the planet had failed, and it often looked as if it was about to, I could have simply gotten back into my ship and flown away. That's very different to the way you had to risk your life to save others around the galaxy."

Jonathan shrugged. "Your brother did the same."

She looked at Craig again. "Different planets, different risks, different rewards."

"We're supposed to be silent," Craig said tightly.

Tammy shrugged. Jonathan pulled out his comms and started to scroll through it. I shut my eyes and tried to relax. Then I worried that I might fall asleep. I didn't know if I snored or not, but I really didn't want to find out by starting to snore in front of a room full of suspects in a murder investigation.

The next time the door opened, the bot asked Honey to go with it.

"Wish me luck," she told us before she followed it out of the room.

Ava was next. As she left the room, Tammy spoke again.

"What's the logic behind the order in which we're being questioned?" she asked Craig.

He shrugged. "It made sense for them to start with the widow and the daughter. I assume Howard went next because he's in one of the most expensive cabins on the ship. No doubt he insisted that Honey and Ava follow him."

"So who will be next?" Tammy asked.

"Probably anyone who is left who had a connection to the dead man," Craig said.

"That might be me, then," Iris said. Her voice sounded slightly rusty, as if she rarely used it.

"You knew the dead man?" Tammy asked.

Iris nodded. "We were friends. We'd been friends for many years. I'm going to miss him terribly."

"How did you happen to meet Carl Seintruber?" Craig asked.

"He came to my planet to shoot a documentary about us and our languages. I was given the job of speaking to him. I was meant to try to dissuade him from doing his documentary. If I couldn't manage that, then I was tasked with getting him to give a fair and honest account of our planet and our languages."

"Did you manage to do either?" Craig asked.

She flushed. "Carl made a documentary. I feel that it was fair and honest. It revealed a great deal about our planet and our languages, especially Nado, to the rest of the galaxy, but nothing in it was negative."

I found myself nodding. I'd screened that documentary back in the days when I'd been obsessed with Nado. I'd loved it.

"So you've been friends with Carl ever since?" Tammy asked.

She nodded. "We've been close friends ever since."

"Does that mean you know his daughter as well?" Craig asked.

Iris shook her head, her hands fluttering in front of her. "I only met Laresta after I arrived on the *Lady Elizabeth*. Carl introduced us just a few days go."

"You've known the man for how long?" Craig asked.

"Thirty years, maybe longer."

"And you'd never met his daughter?"

She shrugged. "We were simply never in the same place at the same time. I travel a great deal, working as a reporter for my planet. Obviously, Carl also travels a great deal, doing what he does. For many years, Laresta was in school, of course. Carl always thought that it was best for her to be in one place, getting an education, rather than taking her traveling with him with a team of tutors."

The door opened again. "Iris JaKay," the bot said.

She slowly got to her feet.

"You should know that I'm fluent in Nado," the bot said.

She smiled at him and then moved her hands in a flurry of gestures. The bot hummed and whizzed and then made an odd popping noise.

"You should know that I'm familiar with Nado," the bot said. "I suggest you keep your hands still while we talk."

"I don't know that I can do that, but I'll try," Iris replied as she followed the bot out of the room.

"Anyone want a picture?" Troy asked.

"Did you know Carl?" Craig asked him.

Troy shrugged. "Our paths crossed from time to time over the years."

"Didn't he marry Zarina on Val Segas?" Tammy asked. "I don't suppose you photographed their wedding?"

Troy shook his head. "They only got married last year. I wasn't on Val Segas at that time."

"So where did your paths cross?" Craig asked.

"I shot thousands of weddings on Val Segas during the time that I lived there. Carl was a guest at some of them. I also did a shoot for Laresta once. She was putting together a portfolio. I spent an afternoon following her around Val Segas, taking pictures that were meant to look like candid shots."

"When was that?" Tammy asked.

"Maybe five years ago. More or less."

"Did she kill her father?" Craig asked.

Troy looked shocked. "I have no idea. Surely his death was an accident. He fell asleep on the toilet. It happens."

Craig nodded. "Sure, yeah, it happens. But usually, when it happens, the person sitting on the toilet has his or her pants down around his or her ankles."

Troy gasped. "He was fully clothed," he said. "Who sits on a toilet with their pants on?"

"That's a good question," Craig said.

"Troy Dyffryn. We are ready to take your statement," the bot said as it flew back into the room. "And we need all of the photos that you've taken today as evidence."

Troy sighed. "Most of them are terrible, anyway," he said as he got up and walked out of the room behind the bot.

"And then there were four," Tammy said.

Jonathan nodded. Craig scowled.

"How did you end up here with Jonathan?" Tammy asked me.

I felt my cheeks flood with color.

"We met over a dead body," Jonathan said.

Tammy raised an eyebrow. "Alan Royce? Craig told me about that one. And the others, for that matter. There seem to be a lot of dead bodies popping up on this ship. That's one of the reasons why I'm here."

"I can take care of myself," Craig growled.

Tammy laughed. "But you know I can't stop myself from worrying about you."

"You have an entire planet to worry about."

"I have an entire government in place to look after that planet. They don't need me. Not all the time, anyway. Besides, I'm on my way back there now. Just in a more leisurely way than I usually travel."

The door opened again. "Tammy Martelle," the bot said.

"I thought for sure you'd be next," Tammy said to Craig as she got to her feet. "You knew the dead guy. I didn't."

As the door shut behind her and the bot, Jonathan looked at Craig. "You knew Carl?" he asked.

Craig shrugged. "Not well."

I thought Jonathan would ask more questions, but he simply nodded and then went back to scrolling on his comms. The bot came for Craig a short while later.

"Just us now," Jonathan said.

"You should be the one conducting the interviews," I said.

"I'll get the captain to share them with me if necessary. Right now we don't even know that Carl was murdered."

"He was sitting in the bathroom of an unused cabin during a fire-control systems test. That's odd."

"That is odd, but that doesn't mean he was murdered. Maybe he went in there to meet with someone, but the person never turned up. Or maybe he went in there and just had a heart attack or something."

"I didn't think that rich people had heart attacks."

"Modern medical scanners make it highly unlikely, but sometimes people skip their scans or ignore the medical advice they're given."

I sighed. "So he probably didn't die of natural causes."

"I would imagine that he died from a lack of oxygen. Whether he died when the oxygen was removed from the cabin during the fire system test or prior to that is another matter."

"Colonel Brazee?" the bot asked.

"Why don't you interview Diana next?" Jonathan asked. "I can wait."

The bot buzzed and beeped and then let out a small noise that sounded like a fart.

"Diana Dunn? We're ready for you now," the bot said.

"Thanks," I said to Jonathan as I stood up.

"Not a problem," he told me.

I followed the bot into the hallway and then into the cabin next door. Shawn Inmon was sitting on a couch. There were two chairs opposite him. He looked at me and grinned.

"Peggy, hey, what are you doing here?" he asked.

FIVE

I swallowed a sigh. For some reason Shawn always got my name wrong. At least the bot probably knew who I was.

"This witness is Diana Dunn," the bot said.

Shawn frowned. "I thought her name was Peggy. Isn't Diana Dunn the woman who keeps finding all the dead bodies?"

"Yes, this is Diana Dunn. She found the body of Alan Royce in Alpha Sector. In Beta Sector, she discovered the bodies of..."

"Okay, maybe we could just get on with it?" I asked, interrupting the bot's sad recitation.

"Sure," Shawn said. "Yeah, let's get on with it."

The bot whirred and then chirped twice. "Please take a seat."

I sat down on one of the chairs. The bot slowly lowered itself until it was hovering just an inch above the other chair. Presumably, that was to make me feel more comfortable, as if we were all just sitting together, having a chat, but instead I felt slightly unnerved, unable to tear my eyes away from the inch of space between the bottom of the bot and the chair.

"Please detail any and all contact you have ever had with the dead man," the bot said.

I frowned. "I'm not even totally sure who is dead. I mean Zarina said it was her husband, but I only know her name because Jonathan told me who she was. Was the dead man Carl Seintruber?"

The bot beeped several times. "The body has been identified as Carl Seintruber, content producer. Please detail every contact you have ever had with the man."

"I've watched some of his content," I said. "I love some of the older things he produced. But that isn't actually contact. I never met the man."

"He was a really good content producer," Shawn said. "We were honored when he chose the *Lady Elizabeth* for his passage to Val Segas. And we were more than happy to let him have space on C Deck to shoot screen footage and immedieos."

"As I understand it, he paid for the privilege," I said.

Shawn shrugged. "I have people that handle the finer details."

The bot clicked loudly. "Tell us about your relationship with Zarina Seintruber."

"I've never met her. We were not introduced this morning, and we never spoke to one another, at least not that I recall."

"What about Laresta Seintruber?"

"Same answer. In fact, the answer is the same for just about everyone who was here this morning. This might go faster if I tell you the names of the people I did know who were at the fire safety test."

"Proceed," the bot said after a few beeps.

"Jonathan Brazee was the person who invited me to come to the test."

"How do you know Colonel Brazee?" Shawn asked.

I stared at him. "The colonel was with me when Alan Royce's body was found," I said. "And he's helped me on a number of other occasions when I've been involved in murder investigations."

"Who else do you know?" the bot asked.

"Becca Syme, because she's the ship's Chief Medical Officer."

"Becca's awesome," Shawn said. "She's one of my favorite people in the entire world. I wish I could clone her and have a dozen Beccas on the medical team. I'd probably marry one of the clones, too, just so I could have my own personal Becca around all the time."

"The cloning of organic species is illegal throughout the entire galaxy," the bot said. "The planet of Fordayne does allow some genetic manipulation, but even they do not permit the cloning of living organisms."

Shawn shrugged. "I should talk to my father. He probably has a lab somewhere that could do the job."

"It's illegal," I said flatly.

"But think how much better the galaxy would be if we everyone could have his or her own Becca. I'm going to have to think about how to make this a reality."

"Who else do you know?" the bot asked.

"I know Troy."

"Because you found his body when he was attacked."

"Because he took some pictures of my cat for me before he was attacked."

"What about Howard Howard?"

"Yeah, my social circle doesn't include famous content

producers like Howard Howard," I said. "It also doesn't include makers like Honey Phillips or Ava Ross."

The bot hummed for a short while. "What about Iris JaKay? Had you met her before today?"

I shook my head.

"Please respond audibly so that your response can be properly recorded."

"I never met her before today. I didn't properly meet her today."

"What about Craig Martelle?"

"We'd met before," I said.

"He and Colonel Brazee have a lot of history together," Shawn said.

"Do they?" I asked, trying not to sound as eager to hear about it as I really was.

Shawn shrugged. "They served in Space Corps together. As I understand it, Colonel Brazee is the reason why Craig never made it past the rank of captain. Or maybe it was Craig's fault that Jonathan never made it to general. It's one or the other."

"What about Tammy Martelle?" the bot asked.

I shook my head and then sighed. "No. I'd never met her before today."

"Were you aware that she was on the ship?" the bot asked.

"No. Not at all. I didn't know any of the people who were at the test were on the ship, aside from the ones I'd previously met."

"I thought everyone knew about Howard," Shawn said. "Why would parents name their child Howard Howard?"

"I have no idea," I said.

"He's been making immedieos all over the ship since we left Cenclare. I can't believe you didn't know," Shawn said.

"I had no idea."

"We have reason to believe that Carl Seintruber was murdered," the bot said. "Who do you think killed him?"

I stared at the bot. "I have no idea," I said eventually. "I didn't know the man. I have no idea who might have wanted him dead."

"Lots of people," Shawn said in a conspiratorial whisper. "For a start, he and Howard were rivals."

"But content creation is a huge field. Surely there was plenty of room for both of them," I said.

Shawn shrugged. "In the galaxy, sure, but they are both on the *Lady Elizabeth* at the moment. Or were. Now only Howard is on the ship. I mean, technically, Carl is still on the ship, but only his body is here. His soul has gone to the next plane of existence. Do you believe in existence planes?"

It took me a moment to catch up to the man's rambling train of thought. "What does being on the *Lady Elizabeth* have to do with content creation?" I asked.

Shawn blinked at me. I could almost see him struggling to rewind the conversation in his head to try to figure out what I was asking.

"Oh, that," he said eventually. "Yeah, so they were both trying to create content in the same place. And they were both really vocal, complaining about having to share the space. Like it's my fault that we had to put passengers in some of the cabins down here. That wasn't my fault."

"So he and Howard were fighting?" I asked.

Shawn nodded. "And so were Carl and Zarina, but I never told you that."

I frowned. While I was curious about the various suspects, I really shouldn't encourage Shawn to gossip about the other passengers on the ship. "What were they fighting about?" I couldn't stop myself from asking.

"Zarina wanted a baby. Carl didn't want any more kids. But then Carl changed his mind. He told Zarina she could have a baby once they got to Val Segas. They were going to use a growing tube. Zarina wasn't going to carry the baby herself."

"Most women don't these days."

Shawn nodded. "And good for them. I can't imagine what it would feel like to carry a baby around inside of me. I don't even like holding them when they're on the outside. Babies are kind of nasty little things, really."

I had no idea how to respond to that.

"Carl told me that he didn't want Laresta to know about the baby. He knew she'd be upset when she found out."

"Because she wanted to be an only child?" I asked.

"Because she wanted to be the only heir. Carl left behind a fortune. I'm sure Laresta wants to get her hands on as much of it as possible. Of course, she's going to have to fight Zarina for every credit."

"I didn't think people fought over inheritances any longer."

Every planet in the galaxy had laws in place that required every adult to file an inheritance plan on an annual basis. They could be changed and updated at any time, but a document had to be submitted at least once a year. I'd laughed every year when I'd filed mine, because I had nothing of value to leave to anyone, but I was still required to file.

"The very wealthy do. I'm sure my entire family will fight endlessly when my father dies. I have far too many brothers and sisters who are all going to want some part of the estate. And my father has a bad habit of forgetting about some of his children sometimes. I can't tell you how many times I've contacted him and not gotten a reply because he'd forgotten all about me."

"I'm sorry," I said, feeling genuine pity for the man.

He shrugged. "It's not like we ever spent any time together. I've only been in the same room with him six times in my life."

While I wanted to hear more about Shawn's unfortunate upbringing, I was also tired and hungry.

"Is there anything else?" I asked the bot.

"Who do you think killed Carl Seintruber?" the bot asked again.

I frowned. "It sounds as if Shawn has a better idea of that than I do."

"It could have been anyone," Shawn said. "He and Craig worked together for a while. Maybe Craig killed him. Or maybe Tammy did it. She's ruthless, you know. You can't build a planet from nothing without being ruthless."

"What about Iris JaKay?" the bot asked.

I wasn't sure if it was asking me or Shawn. Of course, Shawn assumed the question was for him.

"She seems nice. I can't understand what she's doing with her hands all the time, but she seems nice anyway. She's a traveling reporter for the Nadoians. I've never been to Nado. I'm told it's a nice planet, though. Maybe we should stop there on our way to Val Segas. I wouldn't mind extending the trip for a few sectors. What do you think?" he asked me.

"I think it would be good to get to Val Segas as quickly as possible."

Shawn laughed. "Then you're on the wrong ship. This is a luxury experience, not a fast one. If you're in a hurry, there are express shuttles that can get you there a lot faster. You'd just have to shuttle-hop your way across the galaxy."

"The ship's course is set," the bot said. "It cannot be altered."

Shawn laughed. "Do you know who I am? I can change anything I want to change."

"Are we finished here?" I asked.

The bot buzzed. "Please tell me everything that happened today, starting with the time you woke up."

Shawn sighed. "I woke up at ten and ordered breakfast in bed. We've been through this before, though."

"Ms. Dunn, please tell me everything that happened today," the bot said.

I told the bot about getting up and feeding Singer before going to the restaurant for breakfast. Then I told it about working on my course until Jonathan knocked. Talking about what came next was more difficult, but I did my best to talk about everything that had happened once we arrived on C Deck right up to when I'd walked into this cabin and sat down.

"I hate when people die," Shawn said. "Even though I know that they continue to exist, just on a different existence plane, it's quite sad."

"It is sad," I said.

"Do you believe in existence planes?" Shawn asked again.

"I don't know much about them."

He nodded. "My father has a team of people working to prove that they're a real thing. He wants to make sure that he has everything arranged before he leaves this plane for the next one. He's worried that if he doesn't have things arranged properly, he might be poor in his next plane."

"Imagine that," I said softly.

"I hope Carl is happier on his next plane. He wasn't very happy here – not lately, anyway."

"That's a shame."

"He kept complaining about Howard and about Zarina. Laresta was a problem, too. She enjoys making immedieos, but she wasn't interested in any of Carl's older work. He left behind a huge legacy of amazing content. Carl wanted her to appreciate his work, but she didn't."

"I don't think that's a motive for murder," I said, mostly to myself.

"Murder? I'm not sure Carl was murdered," Shawn said.

"That's for Becca to determine," I said.

"I'm sure she'll find the right answer. She's amazing," Shawn replied.

"Are we done?" I asked the bot.

"I make the decision here," Shawn said.

"Are we done?" I asked him.

He shrugged and looked at the bot. "Are we done with Peggy?"

I swear I heard the bot sighing in frustration, an emotion it wasn't supposed to have.

"I have no additional questions for Diana Dunn," the bot said. "I might have more questions for her in the future, as the investigation continues."

Shawn nodded. "Yeah, we might have more questions later. As we investigate. That's what we're going to do. Investigate the death."

"Great," I said as I stood up. "I'll go back up to A Deck now, then."

"Please do not talk to the other passengers about what happened here today," the bot said. "We are not releasing any information about the man's death at the moment."

I nodded.

"Or about the safety test," Shawn said. "Obviously, everything went great, but we'd like to keep everything that happened with the test quiet for, um, security reasons."

"I won't say anything to anyone," I said.

"Great. Thanks for answering our questions. Take care," Shawn said.

I headed for the door.

"Let's talk to Diana Dunn next," Shawn said to the bot. "She's found lots of dead bodies. She probably knows exactly what happened to Carl."

"We've already interviewed Ms. Dunn," the bot said. "The only person left to interview is Colonel Jonathan Brazee."

Shawn frowned. "I'm a little afraid of him. He looks as if he could break me in two."

"I'm sure he could," the bot said before it flew over to the door.

I'd been trying to get the door to open and failing. The bot tapped a code into the panel next to the door. The door slowly slid open.

In the corridor, I took several deep breaths before I turned and walked to the elevators. I pushed the button and then paced back and forth while I waited. Part of me was tempted to walk down the corridor to where we'd found the body before the ship had even left Alpha Sector. I knew there wouldn't be anything to see, but it was still tempting. Of course, somewhere beyond the spot where we'd found the body were the cabins where the murderers were being kept until we arrived at Val Segas. Even if they were safely locked inside their cabins, I didn't want to get any closer to them than I had to. I pushed the button again.

When the elevator arrived, the doors only opened halfway. I squeezed between them and then pushed the button for A Deck.

"Please scan your comms," a voice said.

I slid my wrist over the scanner. It beeped several times before the car began to move. When the car stopped, the doors opened.

"This is B Deck," I said.

"Your ticket is for B Deck," the elevator told me. "Please disembark now."

"But my cabin is on A Deck," I protested.

The elevator didn't respond. When I tried to push the button for A Deck, the entire panel switched off. I sighed and then walked out of the car. I'd been on B Deck before, so I wasn't surprised to see the row of vending machines right outside the elevators. I walked over and bought myself a slice of chocolate cake before trying the elevators again.

This time, when I pushed the button for A Deck, I wasn't asked to scan. Instead, the car rose silently, carrying me to A Deck. I jumped out of the car as soon as the doors started to open. Then I quickly made my way back to my cabin, clutching my cake. Singer looked up from her pillow as I walked into the cabin.

"Meerwwww," she said sympathetically.

"It was awful," I told her. "They started a fire and then the bots couldn't put it out. And then we found a dead guy in the bathroom."

I picked her up and held her close. I could feel her purring against my chest as I sat down in the nearest chair.

"I should cry," I said. "I should feel like crying. A man is dead." I thought for a minute. "Mostly, I feel like crying because I thought I might get burned alive. The bots were useless. What happens if there's a real fire?"

I glanced up at the sprinklers on my ceiling. "They

probably aren't even connected to anything," I muttered as I squeezed my eyes shut.

Singer purred in my ear as I sat and tried to take deep breaths in an effort to calm myself. It helped a little bit, at least.

"Lunch," I said after several minutes. "You need lunch, too."

Singer nodded.

I put her on the floor and then went to the cupboard where I kept all of Singer's supplies. I gave her a pouch of her favorite food to thank her for helping me feel better. Then I sat back down and tried to decide what I wanted to do for lunch.

"I'm not really hungry, but I'm also starving," I told Singer.

She looked up from her bowl and seemed to shrug her tiny shoulders at me.

"Do cats have shoulders?" I asked.

I thought about asking my smart cube but decided I couldn't be bothered. It didn't really matter. Singer ran to the door a moment before someone knocked.

"Hi, Jonathan," I said before I opened it.

He laughed. "She always knows it's me," he said before he picked up Singer and gave her a snuggle.

"She does."

"We need to talk. Have you had lunch?"

I shook my head. "I just got back. How did you get through questioning so quickly? I was in there for ages."

"I prepared my statement while I was waiting. The bot scanned it and said it would be in touch if it needed more information. I'd have been out even sooner, but then Shawn started talking."

I laughed. "Did he say anything useful?"

"Does he ever? Let's go to my cabin. We can order lunch and talk privately there."

I hesitated for a second before nodding. "Sure."

SIX

Jonathan's cabin was a short distance from mine. He had an entire suite, with a comfortable living room full of couches and chairs. I followed him there and settled onto one of the couches.

"Order whatever you want for lunch," he said, tapping on the table to bring up the restaurant's menu.

I scanned through the options. "There are things on here that aren't available in the dining room," I said.

He shrugged. "The suites have their own menus. They try to give us more options to make us feel like the extra we paid was worth it."

I looked around the large room. "You have a lot more space than the rest of us."

"And that was worth the credits. I can't imagine what it would be like traveling in one of the cabins on C Deck."

I shuddered. "I thought B Deck was bad, but that room today was unbelievably small. I actually felt a bit of sympathy for the people who are staying on C Deck."

"Even though they're murderers."

"Troy didn't die."

"That's true. But the person who tried to kill him deserves to be on C Deck, regardless."

I nodded. "And now someone else is dead."

"Indeed."

"How well did you know Carl?"

"We'd met," Jonathan said. "Twice. The first time was when he found himself in a bit of trouble on a planet where a coup took place while he was shooting a docudrama about the planet's government. Space Corps had to go in and get him and his crew out safely before they could be arrested for supporting the now-ousted regime."

"Scary."

"All in a day's work. The new government was more sensible than most, really. They didn't want to generate the sort of negative publicity that arresting a man like Carl would have given them. They let us collect everyone and only shot a few lasers at us as we departed."

"They shot at you?"

"The shots were easy enough to evade. That's the sort of flying I grew up doing back on my home planet."

"You used to get shot at on your home planet?"

He laughed. "I used to play boom tag with all of my friends. We'd take our shuttles into low orbit and then shoot at each other with low-level lasers. If you got hit, it made a lot of noise, but it didn't do any damage to the shuttles. From there, I moved on to minjets. Of course, once I joined Space Corps, I learned how to fly just about everything."

"Could you fly the *Lady Elizabeth* if you had to?"

"You could fly the *Lady Elizabeth* if you had to. Modern long-distance ships like this one don't actually get flown. They just get programmed and anyone with any sort of basic computer knowledge could reprogram the system in an emergency."

"I suppose that's good to know."

"Have you ordered lunch?" he asked.

I frowned. "I forgot."

I turned my attention back to the screen built into the table. After a minute, I picked something and tapped my order into the screen. Jonathan leaned over and tapped something for himself before tapping again to make the screen go blank.

"So you rescued Carl from some warring planet the first time you met him. When did you see him the second time?"

"About five years ago, he invited me to a party. I was on vacation on a planet in the Delta Region. He was there, shooting his last long-content hit. After that one opened, he started making immedieos and other short-form stuff instead of long content."

"But what happened at the party?" I asked.

He chuckled. "Nothing much. I walked around and had a drink and some food. At one point, Carl and I crossed paths. He introduced me to everyone as the man who'd flown in, lasers blazing, to rescue him from the middle of a civil war. I laughed it off. One of the men he'd been speaking with started trying to talk me into working with him on a screen of my life. I politely declined and then walked away."

"And you never spoke to Carl again?"

"I said hello to him a few days ago when we passed one another in the corridor here. He told me that he'd been meaning to invite me to dinner, but he'd been too busy to socialize. I told him that he knew where to find me for the next twenty sectors. He laughed and then let himself into his cabin."

"It doesn't sound as if you had a motive for his murder, assuming it was murder."

"I didn't have any motive for his murder, and it definitely was murder. It was a very cleverly done murder at that. Or maybe the killer just got lucky. It's even remotely possible that the killer didn't mean for Carl to die."

"I'm lost."

He laughed. "While I'm not officially investigating Carl's death, I do have access to some information that won't be released to the rest of the passengers."

"But you're going to tell me?"

"Yes, because you've been through a number of murder investigations now. You know how this works. And I want you with me when I talk to each of the suspects."

"I don't want to get involved."

He nodded. "In that case, let's enjoy lunch."

When he tapped on the table, the top slid away. A tray holding our lunches lifted out of the center of the table.

"Do you want something to drink?" he asked as I lifted my plate off the tray.

"Oh, a lemon fizzy, please."

He removed his lunch and then tapped in my drink request as the tray slowly sank back into the table unit. I'd only taken a single bite when the table beeped several times. This time the tray held my lemon fizzy and a coffee for Jonathan.

"This is good," I said after another bite. "I wish I could get this in the dining room."

"You're welcome to have lunch here whenever you want, but I can't promise that the menu won't change from time to time."

I shrugged. "I don't want to bother you."

"We're friends. I always enjoy spending time with my friends."

I chewed slowly while I thought about the man's words.

I wasn't certain that I would have classified our relationship as a friendship, but if it wasn't that, then I had no idea how else to define it. All I knew for certain was that Jonathan was the only person on the ship that I felt I could trust.

"What did you learn from Becca, then?" I asked, sighing.

He grinned. "We don't have to talk about the murder."

"But you knew I'd be curious."

"I hoped you'd be curious. I always appreciate your help with investigations. And this one might be trickier than the others were. The killer this time was very clever."

"In what way?"

"From what Becca has been able to determine, Carl was heavily drugged before his death. She believes that he walked into the bathroom himself, probably accompanied by the killer. She reckons that once he sat down, though, he fell asleep almost immediately."

"And then the killer left him there?"

"It seems so."

"Why?"

Jonathan shrugged. "That's one of the things we need to work out. It's possible that the killer was hoping that the bots would seal the room and remove the oxygen, thus killing Carl. Or maybe the killer just wanted Carl to sleep through the test for some reason. Or maybe the killer assumed that the test would go badly wrong, and that Carl would die in the fire."

I frowned. "That doesn't sound like a clever killer to me. It sounds as if everything was left up to chance."

"It does seem as if things were left to chance. But maybe that's because the killer didn't care if Carl survived or not."

"What do you mean?"

"I mean, maybe the killer wanted Carl dead, but wasn't

in any particular hurry to make it happen. So maybe this was just a first attempt at murder. Or maybe it was a second or third or fourth attempt and we simply don't know about the earlier attempts."

"Why would someone want him to sleep through the fire-control test?"

"That's a good question. I don't know."

"Why was he even at the fire-control test? It was supposed to be a test of the ship's systems. Why does a content producer need to be there? Why does he even want to be there?"

"I think everyone on the ship would have gone to the test if they'd been invited. We're six sectors into the journey and everyone is incredibly bored. As for why he was invited, I suspect Shawn invited both Carl and Howard. He was probably hoping that they'd both get some footage of the fire-control bots sweeping in and putting out the fire quickly and efficiently. Then he would have used the footage on screens around the ship to reassure everyone that InmonCorp is all about passenger safety."

"And instead, the fire nearly got out of control and a man is dead."

Jonathan sighed. "It's something of a nightmare for Shawn, although he doesn't appear to have realized that."

"Maybe it would be good to be stupid."

"There are times when I think that," Jonathan said with a laugh.

"Do you think that Howard will release immedieos of the fire burning out of control and the bots failing to put it out?"

"Definitely, although probably not until after we reach Val Segas. Between now and then, he's going to need to get along with Shawn and Captain Ryder."

"So Carl was drugged and left in the bathroom. The killer knew he might die, or he might just wake up and walk out of the bathroom at some point."

"I'm going to hack into the system to see if I can find any evidence that anything to do with today's test was tampered with. I should start running some scans now, actually, while we wait for dessert to arrive."

"We're having dessert?"

He shrugged. "Take a look at the menu. I think there are things on that menu that also aren't available in the dining room."

I scrolled through the dessert menu, muttering under my breath as I went along. "There are eleven desserts on here that aren't on the regular menu," I said when I was done.

Jonathan looked up from the computer where he was working. "Maybe order only five or six for today. You can try the other five or six next time."

"I'm not going to order five desserts," I said. "But I might order two."

"Everything is already paid for. Get five if you want five."

I shook my head. "Two is plenty for today, but I might start knocking on your door more often."

He walked back over and sat down in his chair. "You never knock on my door uninvited."

I shrugged. "Did you get the scans started?"

"Yeah, and I'm hoping it won't take them long to find something. I suspect the killer has already been at work trying to remove all traces of whatever tampering was done, but hopefully, I'm smarter than the killer."

"I'm pretty sure you are."

As the table beeped to let us know that our desserts had

arrived, Jonathan's computer also beeped. I pulled all three plates off the tray while Jonathan walked over to check the screen.

"Interesting," he said before he walked back to join me.

"What have you found?" I asked.

"The security code to unlock the door to that cabin was changed in the middle of the test," he said. "That's why the bots couldn't get in. They were still using the old code."

"They don't get updated immediately?"

"Cabin security codes aren't supposed to be changeable – not by passengers, anyway. If a member of the crew needed to change a security code, he or she would know to push the change through the system so that the fire and security systems would have that change immediately."

"So how did the code get changed?"

Jonathan shrugged. "The system just shows the change. There isn't any trail back to a device making the change."

"How is that possible?"

"Whoever did it has an unlicensed comms unit."

I stared at him. "But those are illegal. I thought they'd pretty much been eliminated?"

"Yes and no. If you wanted to get your hands on one, you could probably find one somewhere for a price. And it would probably be an old unit with limited capabilities. But if you were, say, a famous content producer with more or less unlimited funds at your disposal, then you'd be able to get ahold of the most modern units being produced today in unlicensed versions."

"I had no idea."

"A lot of content creators prefer to use unlicensed equipment. It lets them work anonymously when they want to."

"So Carl probably had an unlicensed unit."

"Undoubtably. If he hadn't had one years ago, when he needed rescuing from that planet, we never would have known he was in trouble. All of the information coming from the planet on official channels was positive. He was lucky that the leaders of the rebellion didn't find his unlicensed comms when they searched his hotel."

I shook my head. "You're talking about a world that's completely foreign to me."

"Let's just say that it wouldn't surprise me to find out that every person in that room this morning had an unlicensed device with him or her."

"I didn't. I've never even seen an unlicensed device."

He laughed and then tapped on the table. A panel slid open to reveal several comms units.

"You might have seen some," he said, picking one up. "They don't look any different." He handed me the unit.

I turned the unit over in my hands. "Anyone in that room this morning could have had an unlicensed device," I said slowly. "And they could have used that device to change the code on the door. We could all have died in there."

Jonathan shook his head. "We were hours away from death. I could have put the fire out with my jacket if I'd needed to. I wasn't worried."

"I don't understand why the killer changed the code."

There was another beep from the computer on the desk. Jonathan read the screen and then walked back and sat down.

"Someone also spent some time going through the entire protocol for withdrawing oxygen from a cabin," he said. "They didn't change anything, they just studied exactly how the system works."

"It's worrying that the system doesn't check for life forms in the bathrooms in those cabins."

"I agree. I believe that the system isn't supposed to work unless the interior door between the bedroom and bathroom is locked open. That would allow the bots to scan both rooms."

"But that didn't happen today."

"Because no one was supposed to be in that bathroom."

"Someone still should have checked."

"I agree. Obviously."

I sighed. "I suppose whoever drugged Carl and left him in the bathroom can claim that he or she isn't responsible for his death because the system should have detected Carl's presence."

"That's one of the reasons why I said the killer was clever. He or she can claim that the fire upset them so much that they forgot that Carl was in the bathroom. Or maybe claim that they assumed that oxygen would continue to flow to the bathroom, that only the bedroom would be cut off."

"Maybe you should just let Shawn handle this one."

Jonathan laughed. "You know as well as I do that Shawn isn't capable of finding Carl's killer. I'm not sure I'm going to be able to manage it, but I have to try. I'm uncomfortable with the idea that a clever killer is wandering around the ship."

"Where do we, er, you even start?"

"'We' is better. I'm going to need all the help I can get."

"I doubt very much I'm going to be able to do anything."

"People talk to you, though, more than they talk to me. I seem to intimidate people."

"I wonder why," I said sarcastically.

He shook his head. "So do I. I'm just an ordinary guy."

I started to laugh. "If you call rescuing people from

warring planets ordinary, yeah. And that's only one of the stories I've heard about you. According to everyone I meet, you're a legend across the entire galaxy."

"You can't believe everything you hear."

"But most of it is true."

"Maybe. But I'm retired now. None of that matters."

"Maybe not to you, but it matters to other people."

"We need to talk to everyone that was in that room this morning."

"You know better than I do how to accomplish that."

He nodded. "Many of the people who were there are staying in suites. They'll be easy enough to find when we want to talk to them. I want to talk to Becca, too, but she won't want to talk to me."

"She told you that Carl had been drugged."

He grinned. "I never actually said that I talked to Becca."

I frowned. "You hacked into the medical system?"

"I didn't need to hack anything. I have access to all of the ship's systems, thanks to Captain Ryder. He seems to believe that the ship is safer if I know what's happening on board."

"I don't disagree."

"I'm glad to hear that."

"So you want to talk to Becca."

"And Troy, although that's probably a waste of time."

"You should ask him for copies of all of the photos he took."

"I should have access to them. He's supposed to upload everything into the ship's computer, but I'll request them anyway. It's probably best if people don't know that I have access to the systems."

"How did Carl get into that room in the first place?" I asked.

"He and Howard both have cards that allow them to access most of C Deck. They were both using C Deck for making content and for research purposes. According to the ship's computer, Carl was given four access cards for C Deck. Howard was given three."

"And those cards let them into cabins on the deck?"

"The cards let them use the elevators to get to C Deck in the first place. They also give them access to all areas of the deck that are not being used. From what I can determine, the only spaces they couldn't access were the cabins that are occupied and the two cabins where the construction bots are currently working."

"Why cards? Why didn't they just get access programmed into their comms?"

"That's a very good question. One I'd very much like an answer to. If they'd used comms, we'd know exactly who got into that cabin this morning."

"And why so many cards? What did Carl need four cards for?"

"I would imagine he gave one each to Zarina and Laresta. I'm not sure why he needed a fourth."

"Does that mean that Howard gave cards to Honey and Ava?"

"Probably."

"So they all need to be at the top of the suspect list. None of the others could have accessed that cabin this morning."

"Anyone could have been with Carl."

I sighed. "Yeah, okay."

"And Craig can hack his way through any system and

get in anywhere. He'll have at least one unlicensed device with him, and probably more than one."

"What about Tammy?"

"She built her own planet. I've no doubt she's an expert at computer systems."

"Iris? Please tell me that she's just a lovely woman who happened to be in the wrong place at the wrong time."

"As far as I know, she's exactly that, but she was also one of Carl's oldest and dearest friends. If she asked him to take her to C Deck and show her around before the test started, he would have agreed instantly."

"And Troy and Becca both work on the ship, so they both have access to every deck."

"They do. And Troy could easily explain..."

Jonathan was interrupted by a loud knock on the door.

"Are you expecting someone?" I asked.

He shook his head. "Not at all."

He took the unlicensed comms unit out of my hands and put it back in its compartment before tapping to shut the panel. Then he walked to the door and touched the screen next to it. The screen showed what the camera above the door could see.

"Craig and Tammy? What do they want?" I asked.

SEVEN

"Do we want to find out?" Jonathan asked as Craig knocked again.

"You wanted to talk to them anyway."

He made a face. "I thought maybe you could talk to them."

"Someone needs to talk to them."

Jonathan sighed and then pushed the button to open the door, catching Craig with his hand in the air, poised to knock again.

"What took so long?" Craig growled.

"Tammy, it's nice to see you again," Jonathan said.

Tammy laughed. "You just saw me this morning."

"This morning wasn't nice," Craig said. "Invite us in," he said to Jonathan after a quick look up and down the corridor.

Jonathan stepped back. "Come in," he said.

Tammy smiled at me as she walked into the cabin.

"We didn't get to meet earlier," she said. "I'm Tammy Martelle."

"Diana Dunn," I replied.

She nodded. "Craig has told me a lot about you."

I felt myself blushing. "He has?"

"You've had some very unfortunate moments since you boarded the *Lady Elizabeth*."

"That's very true."

"It's a Cubbon anomaly."

"I'm sorry?"

She shrugged. "I study history in my spare time. A Cubbon anomaly is when one person suddenly seems to get caught up in a number of criminal investigations, one after another, even though they themselves are law-abiding and otherwise ordinary people."

Jonathan nodded. "I remember reading an article about that once. It never occurred to me that Diana was experiencing it, though."

"I believe there have to be ten incidents in the space of a year before it can be properly termed a Cubbon anomaly, but you're well on your way there," Tammy told me.

"Maybe this will be the last one and I'll never quite make it to ten," I said hopefully.

"Why is it called a Cubbon anomaly?" Craig asked.

Tammy shrugged. "It's been called that for thousands of years. I believe it dates back to an anomaly that happened on Earth in the years before space travel began, but you know a lot of Earth records have disappeared over the centuries."

"How often does it happen?" I asked.

"If you search the historical records of most planets, you'll usually find at least one Cubbon anomaly there somewhere. Sometimes they aren't identified as such, but they often are. They were more obvious when space travel was less commonplace. Now, as people move around the galaxy, it's more difficult to track events that happen to individuals in the same way."

"If you'd been shuttle-hopping instead of traveling on the *Lady Elizabeth,* no one would have noticed that you keep finding dead bodies," Craig said.

"Except I've found most of them on the *Lady Elizabeth.* Maybe the Cubbon anomaly applies to the ship, not me."

"Maybe you'd like to tell us why you're here," Jonathan said to Craig and Tammy.

The pair exchanged glances.

"I thought maybe we could join forces," Craig said after a minute. "A man was murdered. There are a lot of suspects. I thought maybe we could work together to question all of them and find the killer."

"We want to help," Tammy said. "And we know that you've worked with Captain Ryder and Shawn Inmon on murder investigations before."

Jonathan shrugged. "I want to speak to each of the suspects myself."

Craig nodded. "So do I. But after we've all spoken to all of them, maybe we could compare notes."

"Maybe," Jonathan said flatly.

Craig looked as if he wanted to argue. Tammy gave him a sweet smile.

"We've already learned a few things," she said. "Carl was drugged before he was left in the cabin's bathroom."

"I know," Jonathan said.

"And he died an hour before the fire-control bots sealed the cabin and started removing oxygen," Tammy added.

Jonathan stared at her.

"I don't understand," I said.

"Someone ran a systems test on the oxygen control system in that cabin an hour before the actual test began,"

Tammy said. "It was buried in the long list of tests and protocols that were done before the official test started, but it's there if you know where to look."

"So Carl was already dead before the fire even started," Jonathan said thoughtfully.

"Which means it was definitely murder," Craig said. "We have to assume that the killer was hoping that no one would notice the earlier test that was run which actually killed Carl."

"Surely he or she knew that everything that happened before the fire would be scrutinized," I said.

Tammy shrugged. "There are over a thousand lines of test protocols that took place before the actual test started. Once the test started, the pre-test protocol processes were completely overwritten by the actual test results. It took some digging to find them."

Jonathan glanced over at his computer. Clearly it hadn't dug deep enough yet.

"But surely the killer knew that the time of death would be wrong," I said.

"Perhaps the killer was expecting the test to move more quickly than it did," Tammy said. "Or maybe the killer didn't expect the body to be found until much later. The longer the body was there, the more difficult it would have been for Becca to determine exactly when he died."

I frowned. "Why did Troy open the bathroom door?"

Tammy and Craig exchanged glances.

"That's a very good question," Craig said. "It's on the list of things I want to ask Troy."

"I think it might be best if you leave the investigation to Shawn and Captain Ryder," Jonathan said.

Craig shook his head. "I'm not going to do that. We came to offer to work with you as a courtesy, but whatever your answer, we're going to be doing everything we can to find Carl's killer."

"Why don't you tell me about your relationship with Carl," Jonathan said.

Craig stared at him. I could almost see steam coming out of his ears.

"We'd crossed paths a few times over the years," Craig said eventually. "I was sent to get him off a planet that was experiencing a massive meteor shower once. After that, he interviewed me in order to get background information for something he was producing. We kept in touch occasionally."

"Did you see him on the ship at all?" Jonathan asked.

Craig shook his head. "Not really. We saw each other in passing once or twice, but never actually spoke. Those of us who are staying on B Deck don't really get to mingle with the passengers in the A Deck suites."

Tammy laughed. "You're mingling with me a lot and I have an A Deck suite."

Craig just shook his head.

"What about his wife?" Jonathan asked.

"What about her? I knew he'd gotten married, but I've never met Zarina. I didn't introduce myself to her this morning."

"What about his daughter?" was the next question.

Craig sighed. "I have met Laresta once or twice."

"Once or twice?" Jonathan demanded.

Craig thought for a moment. "Actually, it was three times. The first time was when I did that interview. She was only a child, playing in her father's office while he was working. A few years later I was part of a team that rescued some folks off Splestra before its sun went supernova. Laresta was one of the people we rescued."

"That was a mess," Jonathan said.

"You don't have to tell me that. I was there."

"I hope Laresta was suitably grateful," Tammy said.

Craig's laugh was harsh. "No one was grateful. Every single spoiled rich kid that we picked up on that planet was angry and openly hostile. In some ways we got lucky that we barely made it out alive. We lost one of our escorts. Three solid members of Space Corps lost their lives rescuing the offspring of the rich and famous. That shut up even the whiniest of the complainers, at least."

"Dan Ross was a friend of mine," Jonathan said quietly.

"He was brilliant in a cockpit. When I heard they hadn't made it, I couldn't believe it."

Jonathan nodded. "He wasn't even supposed to be there. He was on assignment – ah, but never mind. Tell me about the other time you met Laresta."

"We bumped into each other on Val Segas a while back. She was there partying with friends. She actually made a point of coming over to talk to me. She said she wanted to thank me for helping get her off Splestra. She also admitted that she hadn't been properly appreciative at the time. I told her that I'd just been doing my job. Then she asked me to be in a few immedieos for her. I just walked away."

"What about Howard Howard?" Jonathan asked.

"I acted as a consultant on one of his series."

"So you know him well."

Craig laughed. "He sent me daily segments to screen. I sent back notes where there were obvious errors in either the science or in the way in which Space Corps operates. Howard's assistant handled everything. I believe I spoke to Howard once, maybe twice, while I worked through over half a dozen segments."

"Did he kill Carl?"

"I don't think so. If he'd wanted Carl dead, he could have found better ways to make it happen. This was too fancy for someone like Howard."

"Did they dislike one another?" I asked.

Craig looked at me. "They were business rivals, although less so since Carl started focusing more on immedieos and less on longer-form content. They often had loud disagreements in public, but I always thought that the fights were primarily for publicity purposes, not because of any genuine rivalry."

"What about Honey and Ava? Did you ever meet them before today?" Jonathan asked.

"Never. I didn't even know who they were. Tammy enlightened me."

Jonathan glanced at Tammy. "I have questions for you, too."

She shrugged. "I might have answers for you."

"What about Iris JaKay?" Jonathan asked Craig.

He frowned. "Is that the Nadoian? I didn't catch her name. And I've never seen her before today."

"Tammy, which of the people who were in the suite this morning do you know?" Jonathan asked.

She grinned. "Captain Ryder, for a start."

"Really?"

"He's been the captain on a couple of other ships I've traveled on. I always make a point of meeting the ship's captain when I board. I've found I get much better service when the staff think I have some connection to the captain."

"Do you think he killed Carl?"

Tammy laughed. "Absolutely not. If he wanted to kill someone, he has access to dozens of methods that would be quick and easy for him. He didn't need to go through all of the fire testing malarkey just to get rid of someone."

"Who else?"

"I knew Carl. Not well, but he shot a few things on my planet. We've also traveled on the same ship together before." She sighed. "Okay, the truth is that we had a bit of a flirtation a few years ago. He took me out for a few nice dinners, and we talked vaguely about becoming more serious. Then he met Zarina. I simply couldn't compete with her. She's decades younger than me, for one thing."

"Does that mean that you knew Zarina before today?"

"We'd met," Tammy said flatly.

"Did she kill Carl?"

"I'd love to think that she did. I don't like her. I knew the day I met her that she was only interested in Carl for his credits, but she was clever enough to hide that fact from Carl. Now she's probably a very rich widow."

"She's pretty successful in her own right," I said, not sure why I felt as if I had to defend a woman I'd never met.

"She's successful because she has Carl's credits behind her. He pays for tons of advertising to send people to her interweb pages. Or rather, he paid. Now she's going to have to try to find someone else to handle the advertising side of her business."

"So you don't like Zarina," Jonathan said. "Noted. What about Laresta?"

Tammy shrugged. "We met a few times while I was, um, friendly with Carl. She wasn't really interested in getting to know me, though. She was busy with her friends and her business. She told me that she didn't care how many credits Carl gave me because she was more than happy to be made to stand on her own two feet in life. We both knew it was a barefaced lie, but I applauded her for making the statement, even if we both knew she didn't mean a word of it."

"Who do you think will inherit Carl's estate?" I asked.

"I suspect he will have split it between Zarina and Laresta, but I can't even begin to guess what share will go to each. I believe Laresta should get a larger percentage, but Zarina put a lot of effort into convincing Carl that she cared. He might have divided things fifty-fifty between them."

"Any chance Laresta killed him?" Jonathan asked.

Tammy shook her head. "She loved her father. He was the only parent she'd ever known, of course. Her mother took off when Laresta was a baby."

"Any chance Laresta's mother is hiding somewhere on this ship?" I asked.

Everyone looked at me. I shrugged.

"Maybe she was still angry about the way Carl treated her. Maybe she decided to come on the *Lady Elizabeth* and kill Carl."

"It's an interesting idea," Craig said, clearly not meaning his words.

"It's worth checking," Tammy said. "It shouldn't be too hard to track Natalie down, even if she's still on Florzonia."

"How well do you know Howard?" Jonathan asked.

Tammy laughed. "Very, very well."

"Tammy," Craig said in a warning tone.

She looked at him and shrugged. "We were a couple for about a year. That was probably a decade ago, maybe more. We had a lot of fun until one day it wasn't fun any longer."

"Did he kill Carl?"

"He and Carl were friendlier in those days. Howard was the one who introduced me to Carl for the first time. That was years before Carl and I became involved, though."

"What changed?" Jonathan asked.

"I don't know that anything really changed. Like Craig said, a lot of their rivalry was for publicity purposes."

"So you don't think Howard killed Carl?"

"I don't, but I haven't totally taken him off my list, either."

Jonathan nodded. "What about Honey and Ava?"

"I'd never met either of them before this morning. And I didn't actually meet them this morning, so I suppose I've never met either of them."

"They weren't working for Howard when you were together?"

"I don't think so, but I didn't meet every member of his team of writers during our year together. One or both of them might have already been part of that team, but neither was a head writer back then."

"And they are now?"

"Oh, they're both past that now. They've both reached named-writer status, where their names get attached to their projects. Not many writers manage to become that successful these days."

"Did either of them have any reason to kill Carl?"

"I can't possibly answer that. I don't know enough about either of them to say. One or both of them might have worked for Carl in the past. Maybe he was romantically involved with one or both of them. There are other possibilities."

"What about Iris?"

"I never met her before today. I found her fascinating, though. I love watching Nadoians talk. They seem to use their hands just to breathe, really. Every word they say seems to expand with those graceful gestures. I once asked a Nadoian to tell me something bad or sad because their gestures are so lovely that I couldn't imagine how a bad or sad thing would look."

"How did it look?" I asked, remembering Iris's cries for help that morning.

"Heartbreakingly sad. I don't know how they do it, but the gestures that they make magnify everything that they say. I was almost in tears watching him talk about a lost puppy. And it was an imaginary puppy, at that."

"What about Becca or Troy?" Jonathan asked.

"I know Becca because I always make sure that I meet the Chief Medical Officer on the ships on which I travel. She's far too smart to work for InmonCorp, but that's another matter."

"Can you see her killing Carl?"

Tammy laughed. "She could have killed him a dozen different ways and not gotten caught. And she could very easily fake the test results she's getting from the autopsy if she had killed him in this rather clumsy fashion."

"It was clever," I said.

"It was overdone. The drug that was used to put Carl to sleep would have killed him at a slightly higher dose. The killer could have just given Carl that dose and then left him to die in his own bed. Getting him to that cabin and putting him in the bathroom only to cut off his oxygen supply was unnecessary theater."

"That's an interesting choice of words," Jonathan said.

She shrugged. "It's been a long time since theater was properly appreciated, but it's an art form that I adore. I've traveled halfway around the galaxy just to see a particular performance with a few especially gifted actors."

"That suggests that someone involved in the screen industry killed Carl," I said.

"They seem the most likely suspects," Tammy said.

"What about Troy?" Jonathan asked her.

She laughed. "Troy doesn't have the computer skills to do what was done to Carl. Besides, he's only just been released from the medical suite. He's weak and tired and not up to planning a murder."

"Did you know Troy before today?"

"Oh, yes. I've been to a lot of weddings, including quite a few on Val Segas. For many years, if you didn't have Troy shoot your wedding photos, you weren't anyone in Val Segas society."

"You don't think he killed Carl?"

"I think, if he'd had access to Carl, he would have asked him for a job. I can't see any reason why he'd want to kill him, even if Carl told him no. Troy can be persistent. He would have just kept trying."

"Are you done questioning us?" Craig asked.

Jonathan shrugged. "For now, unless there's anything else you want to tell me."

"I'll tell you that we're going to investigate the murder to the best of our abilities," Craig said as he got to his feet. "We can take everything we learn to Captain Ryder if you aren't interested."

"I'd be grateful if you would share what you learn with me," Jonathan said to Tammy.

She nodded. "We can do that."

"Thanks."

Craig scowled and then walked to the door. "Let's go," he snapped at Tammy.

She rolled her eyes before getting to her feet.

"Thank you," she said.

"What are you thanking him for?" Craig asked.

"Time," Tammy said. "Although it seems endless on a

long-distance space journey, it's actually a very precious resource."

I couldn't quite make out what Craig muttered under his breath. He opened the door and walked out as Tammy followed. The door slid shut behind them a moment later.

"That was interesting," I said.

"If you say so."

I frowned. "Tammy seems to know just about everyone."

"She does."

Another knock on the door interrupted again.

"I hope they haven't come back," Jonathan said as he walked to the door. He tapped on the screen next to it.

"It's the devastated widow," he said. "I wonder what she wants."

"She doesn't look devastated," I muttered as Jonathan reached for the button to open the door.

EIGHT

"Colonel Brazee, I'm sorry to bother you," Zarina said.

Jonathan shook his head. "It's no bother. I'm very sorry for your loss."

She nodded. "Thank you. I'm, well, devastated, of course. But also confused and more than a little terrified."

"Come in," Jonathan said. He took a step backward. Zarina walked into the room. She stopped when she saw me on the couch.

"I didn't realize you had company," she said.

"Zarina Seintruber, this is Diana Dunn," Jonathan said. "Of course I know who you are, even though technically, we've never been introduced," he said to Zarina.

"Everyone in the galaxy knows who *you* are," Zarina said with a smile.

"Diana and I were just discussing your husband's murder," Jonathan said.

Zarina winced. "I keep hoping that his death was just a horrible accident."

"Have a seat," Jonathan said.

Zarina sat down on the couch opposite me. She sat back

and then closed her eyes. "It might have been an accident. Maybe he started feeling dizzy or unwell, so he went into the bathroom to sit down. And then maybe he had a heart attack or something."

"When was his last complete medical scan?" Jonathan asked.

"He had one a few days before we boarded the *Lady Elizabeth*. Everyone had to have a scan before boarding, or so we were told."

"I believe that's correct," Jonathan said. "Everyone who hadn't had one in the previous six months, anyway."

She nodded. "Carl wasn't very good about keeping up with such things. He was simply very busy, that's all. I used to nag him all the time about it, but he never listened to me. Oh, no. That sounds dreadful. Of course he listened to me. We had a great relationship and communicated very well together. But he didn't like to be reminded that he needed to take care of himself. At his age, scans are recommended every three months. Even with me nagging, he probably only went once a year."

"But he was given clearance to travel across the entire galaxy," Jonathan said.

"He was also told to have himself scanned regularly onboard," Zarina said. "I started nagging him in Chaos Sector to go and see Becca. He never went."

"The sort of blockages that cause heart attacks don't develop that quickly," Jonathan said.

"Then it was an accident," Zarina said. "He probably just sat down for a minute to check something on his comms and fell asleep. He used to do that all the time."

Jonathan shrugged. "Anything is possible, but for the moment, I'm treating his death as suspicious."

"And that idea terrifies me. No one had any reason to

want to kill Carl. He was a brilliant man and a legend in the screen industry. It can't have been murder."

"Let's talk about the people who were on C Deck this morning," Jonathan said. "Maybe we can figure out a motive for one or more of them."

"I barely know most of them," Zarina said.

"It could be argued that you had a motive," Jonathan said.

She shook her head. "I loved my husband very much. We were very happily married. We were even talking about having a baby together. Carl was excited about the idea of being a father again."

"But you do stand to inherit an enormous number of credits," Jonathan said.

She shrugged. "I make a lot of my own credits from my immedieos. I have dozens of sponsors and billions of subscribers to my studio. I'm trying not to think about what's going to happen to all of that, actually. I'm brilliant at making immedieos, but Carl handled absolutely everything else. I don't know how to edit or upload or how to negotiate with sponsors or anything. The only thing I use my comms for is shooting footage, and Carl actually used to do most of the shooting, too."

"You can learn everything you need to know very quickly," Jonathan said.

"I doubt it. I'm hopeless when it comes to computers, really. Which is proof that I didn't kill Carl, of course. Not only did I love him dearly, but I needed him. He was the one who made my business work. I'm probably going to have to hire someone to do all of the things that Carl did for me. That will cut into my income, though."

"But you will be inheriting something from Carl's estate," Jonathan said.

She sighed. "I hope I will. When we first got married, I was legally excluded from Carl's inheritance plan. He wanted to make sure that I was marrying him for the right reasons. He promised that the next time he did an update, he'd include me and that every update after I'd be given a bit more. I have no idea if he actually followed through, though."

"When did he last update his plan?" Jonathan asked.

"Oh, that he did at least monthly. I couldn't talk him into getting a medical scan at all, because he didn't want to think about his own mortality, but he was more than happy to write and rewrite his inheritance plan every single month."

"Did he make many changes each month?"

"He changed a lot of the small beneficiaries constantly. He'd worked with a lot of different people over the years, and he was almost obsessed with the idea of making sure that they were all mentioned in his inheritance plan. He has rooms full of memorabilia from every bit of content he ever made. And he wanted to leave those bits and pieces to the other people who were involved in each of the projects. The problem was people kept dying on him. He used to spend hours going through his list of stuff, assigning and reassigning it to people that he hadn't spoken to in decades."

"So he had reasons for updating the plan regularly."

"Yeah, and I think he really enjoyed it. He used to chuckle to himself as he worked. I could hear him muttering under his breath about how much this person would love being given this thing or how surprised that person would be to be given that thing. Every time someone died, the lists would come back out and he'd get back to work, making changes here, there and everywhere."

"What about the bulk of his estate?" Jonathan asked.

"I expect most of it will go to Laresta."

"Tell us about Laresta," Jonathan said.

"I don't know what to tell you, really. I only met her after Carl and I got engaged. She's around my age, but she seems decades younger. She had a very privileged and sheltered upbringing, especially compared to mine."

"Oh?"

Zarina shrugged. "We were poor. There were six of us. My father didn't work. He'd inherited a few credits from his grandfather and in his own mind he was a wealthy man who didn't need to work for a living. In reality, if we'd had to rely on what he'd inherited we would have starved to death. My mother worked multiple jobs to keep the bills paid and food on the table. My father was tasked with bringing up the children. Mostly, that meant that he ignored us while he watched endless hours of screen."

"I'm sorry," I said.

She glanced at me and then looked back at Jonathan. "There were six of us fighting for that man's attention all the time. I learned very quickly how to get attention. Luckily, there's demand for that skill in the galaxy today."

"I read your bio. You left home at fourteen."

"Fourteen was the legal age on my planet. I moved to Val Segas and started working in content. I worked for Howard for a while."

"Which planet was home?" Jonathan asked.

She shook her head. "There are some things I don't talk about. I'm sure you can find that information with your connections, but I'm not providing it. I tell what I want to tell about my origins, but there are limits."

"There aren't many planets where fourteen is legal age."

"There are twenty-nine. And I came from one of them. And I really don't want to say any more."

"Why not?" I asked, genuinely puzzled by the woman's reluctance to reveal what seemed like quite basic information to me.

Zarina sighed. "My family is still there. I changed my name and buried my past identity when I moved to Val Segas. I also changed as much of my appearance as I could afford to change. I don't want any of them to realize who I've become. They'd just demand credits. Some of them would probably start putting out immedieos themselves to try to trade in on my success. I want nothing whatsoever to do with any of them."

Jonathan nodded. "So you haven't had any contact with your family since you left your home planet?"

"I have not. And I very much want to keep it that way."

"But we were talking about Laresta," he said.

"I don't know her well. And I don't like her. And I know I shouldn't say that, but I don't. She's been given every advantage in life, but she still wants to be given more and more all the time. I suppose it no longer matters. She's about to inherit a fortune. She'll never have to work again."

"Did she have to work previously?" I asked.

"That's a good question," Zarina said. "I don't think she needed to make credits, not in the same way that I've always needed to. I think she worked to prove to her father that she could be just as successful as he had been. In some ways, I'm a bit sympathetic, really, because it can be difficult, being a Seintruber. People have very high expectations."

"But she was a very successful immedieo creator," Jonathan said.

"She did okay. Mostly because of her father. He shot

and edited everything for her. And he had a wonderful eye for what would get attention."

"Did he do everything for her?" Jonathan asked. "Or does Laresta do some of the work herself?"

'I have no idea. That was between her and Carl."

"Can you think of any reason why she might have wanted to kill him?"

Zarina sighed dramatically. "She was his daughter. They fought now and again, mostly over credits. She was constantly asking him for more and more things – a faster personal shuttle, new clothes, jewelry, and trips. I can't even tell you about the trips she wanted to take. She wanted to see the entire galaxy, and she wanted her father to pay for it. Except mostly she wanted to visit beach planets and vacation world planets and shopping planets. She wasn't really interested in the more ordinary planets that make up most of the galaxy."

"Most people aren't," Jonathan said.

"But that's where the stories are," Zarina said. "I love visiting a random planet and talking to its residents. I can get hundreds of immedieos from their stories. There's nothing interesting about some woman sitting on the beach on Caboluxous. She's on vacation from some dead-end job she probably hates. Maybe she's there with her boyfriend or her husband. Or maybe her girlfriend or her wife. They'll be fighting over their plans or the food. It's all the same. I know because I tried to get some good footage on Caboluxous and couldn't get anything I deemed worth my time. Of course, Laresta came back to the ship with hundreds of barely watchable immedieos."

"What have you been doing on C Deck?"

Zarina sighed. "I haven't been doing much of anything down there. But Laresta has been having a wonderful time shooting clips all over the place on C Deck. She's done some where she's pretended that she's actually staying in one of those cabins. Basically it's just five minutes of her complaining about how small the cabin is, but for some reason some of her viewers seemed to enjoy them."

"Do you have an access card for the deck and the cabins down there?"

She nodded. "Carl gave me one when we first started working there, and I have shot some footage. Sometimes it's just nice to have a quiet space to work in. When we first started working on C Deck, we were usually the only people down there. We used to see the construction bots going in and out of a few rooms, but otherwise, it was just me and Carl and Laresta."

"When did Howard start using the space, too?" Jonathan asked.

"At some point in Beta Sector. We were in one of the cabins one afternoon when we heard voices in the corridor. That was so unusual that we stopped shooting to see what was happening."

"And what was happening?"

"Howard was touring the deck. He was with Shawn and Captain Ryder and those two women who work with him. Howard looked surprised when he saw us. He and Carl had a brief conversation before we went back into the cabin and they carried on walking."

"Was Carl upset that Howard was going to be using the space, too?"

She shrugged. "Both men made a big deal out of complaining about it, but I'm pretty sure it was mostly for show. They'd both paid for what was supposed to be exclusive access, but it was a huge space with plenty of cabins and other spaces for both groups to use without getting in each other's way. If Howard had been trying to shoot a full-blown long-form story down there, it would have been a different matter, but the stuff he has been doing down there didn't need a lot of space."

"What is he doing?" Jonathan asked.

"I'm not sure, really. We all did our best to stay away from one another, but when I did see him, he was usually shooting one or the other of those two women just talking to the camera. I suspect he's making some sort of documentary about them, but I could be wrong."

"Can you think of any reason why Howard might have killed Carl?"

She slowly shook her head. "They were business rivals, but not really. Howard does long-form stuff. Carl gave up doing that sort of thing decades ago. I think they continued the illusion that they were rivals because it got them both some publicity. And publicity matters a lot in our business, no matter what sort of content you're producing."

"What about Honey Phillips or Ava Ross?"

"I barely know either of them. Honey wrote a few of the scripts for things that I made for Howard when I worked for him. We talked a few times during shooting, but just casual conversation. I think Ava wrote one thing that I did, but I don't think she was around when we were actually shooting. I met her at a party or two at Howard's during the years I worked with him, but again, all of our conversations were casual."

"Can you think of any reason why either of them might have killed Carl?"

She shook her head. "I don't think either of them knew Carl. We used to see them in the private bar for the passengers in the suites from time to time. They were always with Howard. Carl used to wave. Howard used to wave back.

Howard never bothered to come over and introduce us to his friends. Of course, Carl never bothered to walk over to meet them, either."

"Is it possible that one of them had some sort of history with Carl?" I asked.

"Carl would have told me if he knew either of them. He used to tell me stories about his past lovers, girlfriends, and enemies. We didn't have any secrets from each other."

"People change. Maybe he knew one of them years ago and in the years since, she's changed her appearance," I said.

"Maybe, but they're writers. They don't usually appear on screen in anything. They don't need to worry about their appearance."

"Unless they wanted to change their identity," I suggested.

Jonathan patted my arm. "What about Iris?" he asked.

"She's fascinating. I want to interview her, but I don't think an immedieo is the best place for it. I've never done any long-form stuff myself, but I'd love to do a long-form interview with her – maybe an hour. Except I would probably just sit and watch her talk. Her hands are magical."

"She and Carl were friends."

Zarina nodded. "Which is why I never asked her for an interview. Carl didn't like the idea. He wanted her to have privacy. Of course, he'd interviewed her years ago. I suggested doing a sort of update to the documentary he'd made all those years ago, but he didn't like that idea, either."

"And as far as you know, they were still friends?"

"Iris had dinner with us last night. They talked endlessly about people I'd never heard of before – people who'd been involved in the documentary that Carl made and other people who'd crossed their paths over the years."

"How boring for you," I said.

"Carl enjoyed wandering down memory lane. At least this time he had someone to talk with who shared some of his memories. Often, he just talked to me. I couldn't do much more than nod and smile while he talked on and on and on."

"So you can't think of a motive for Iris?" Jonathan asked.

"I can't think of a motive for anyone."

"Do you know Craig or Tammy Martelle?"

"Not really."

"What does that mean?"

"I don't know Craig."

Jonathan frowned. "But you know Tammy?"

"We'd met."

"And?"

She sighed. "She didn't like me. She immediately assumed that I was only interested in Carl for his credits. I'm pretty sure she was angling to become the next Mrs. Seintruber herself, actually. Maybe that gave her a motive for his murder. Do you think that she hated him for not marrying her?"

Jonathan shrugged. "Do you think she was in love with Carl?"

Zarina laughed. "Oh, goodness, no. I think she thought marrying Carl would be useful to her. They were friends. I'm pretty sure she liked him, but that woman isn't capable of love. Which is probably why she didn't recognize it when she saw me with Carl."

"That's everyone who was at the fire safety test this morning, aside from the crew members who were there," Jonathan said. "Do you know any of them?"

"I know Captain Ryder, because he took us on a tour of the entire ship a few days after we left Cenclare. We also used to see him in the private bar from time to time."

"Did he get along well with Carl?"

"He was always perfectly polite to me and Carl. I can't imagine why he'd want to kill anyone at all, really."

"What about Becca?"

"She's wonderful. I've been to see her a few times and she was amazing both times. I don't know that Carl had ever met her, though."

"And Troy?"

"The guy with the camera? He came into the private bar one night and tried to take a few pictures. Captain Ryder threw him out. It was still sad when he got attacked, of course."

Jonathan nodded. "Can you think of anything that might help us find your husband's killer?"

She took a deep breath and then shuddered. "I keep thinking about Laresta," she said. "She's going to inherit a fortune. What if she killed her father to get that fortune?"

"That's certainly one possibility," Jonathan replied.

Zarina slowly shook her head. Then she got to her feet. "I need to go and rest. And cry. Mostly, I need to cry."

Jonathan walked her to the door. "I'm going to send Becca to check on you," he said.

"I'm okay. Desperately sad, but okay. Angry and scared and confused and lonely, but okay."

"I'm still sending Becca."

"Thanks. And thank you for your time. If Carl was murdered, I want you to find the killer and put him or her away for a very long time."

"I'll do my best."

She nodded before tapping the button to open the door. Before she stepped into the corridor, she looked up and down the hall.

"Thanks again," she said before walking away.

Jonathan sat down with his comms. "I'm just sending Becca a message," he told me.

"Sure," I said.

"And now, we have work to do," he said as he slipped his comms back into his pocket.

"You might. I'm not getting involved."

"You're already involved."

I sighed. "What are you planning next?"

"I thought I'd head to the private bar for a drink."

"It's the middle of the afternoon."

"And?"

"I don't usually drink until after dinner."

"Time is irrelevant when traveling, especially long-distance. Let's go."

"Who do you expect to find there?"

"No one in particular. I want to talk to the bartender, though. I want to get his impression of everyone involved."

We walked the short distance to the small bar that was for the exclusive use of the passengers occupying suites on the ship. Jonathan scanned his wrist unit on the panel next to the door. It slid open. We walked into the dimly lit space that was filled with artificial smoke.

"Or we could talk to Laresta," Jonathan said, nodding at the woman who was sitting at a table in the corner.

There was a man with her, and judging by the number of empty glasses on the table, they were both drinking heavily. Laresta looked around and spotted Jonathan.

"Colonel Breeeeeeeezzzzzeeeeeeee," she shouted. "Come and tell my new best friend that I'm telling the truth about this morning."

NINE

Jonathan and I exchanged glances. I followed him across the room to the table where Laresta was sitting.

"Oh, you brought your friend, yay," Laresta said. "I'm Laresta. Hi."

"Diana Dunn," I said.

"Great. I won't remember that in an hour. This is Gerald...Jack... Justin, something," she said waving at the man sitting across from her.

"It's Jeremy," the man said, nodding at me. He looked to be in his thirties, with dark hair and a thin moustache that reminded me of a fuzzy caterpillar perched on his upper lip.

"Jonathan Brazee," Jonathan said.

"I know," Jeremy replied. "Everyone knows who you are."

"Sit, sit, sit," Laresta said. "We were just talking about this morning."

"I'm sorry for your loss," I said as I sat down between Laresta and Jeremy.

Jonathan walked around Jeremy to sit opposite me while Laresta waved a hand.

"I'm too drunk to be sad," she said. "Becca gave me something. She said not to mix it with alcohol, but I still felt really sad, so I thought I'd have just one drink."

I looked at the collection of glasses on the table.

Laresta laughed. "Yeah, okay, that was a while ago. I might have had more than one. Or two. Or whatever number comes after two."

Jonathan frowned at Jeremy. "How are you finding the *Lady Elizabeth?*" he asked.

Jeremy looked surprised. "It's fine. I don't enjoy long-distance space travel, but sometimes I don't have a choice. I need to get to Val Segas, and this was one of the most affordable options for getting there."

"What do you do?"

"I'm a cross-galaxy import and export specialist. I help small businesses find markets for their products on planets throughout the galaxy."

Jonathan nodded. "Small businesses?"

Jeremy shrugged. "I have a few larger clients. One of them was kind enough to pay for my passage to Val Segas. If he hadn't, I'd be down on B Deck, hating my life right now."

"He must really like working with you to put you in a suite," Jonathan said.

"Yeah, well, he works with InmonCorp a lot, so he was able to negotiate a suite for me at a substantial discount. I suspect my suite cost him less than a B Deck cabin would have cost me if I'd had to pay for it myself."

"Interesting," Jonathan said.

"He's in here every day," Laresta said. "But I never talked to him before today."

"I'm not here every day," Jeremy said. "But there isn't much else to do on the ship, really. I thought there would be more activities and things, but there isn't much to do besides eat and drink."

"He's been in here every time I've been in here," Laresta said. "Except every time I've been in here, I've been with my father. And we kept to ourselves."

"You knew who her father was, didn't you?" Jonathan asked the man.

He nodded. "I'm a huge fan of some of his work, mostly the Underwater World series."

Laresta laughed. "My father hated that series. He was between jobs and willing to do just about anything when he was offered the first one. He shot the entire thing over a long weekend and edited it in half a day. He never imagined it was going to find a fan base, especially not an obsessive fan base."

"That first movie is a classic," Jeremy said. "It's raw and elemental and intense and brilliant."

"When he agreed to do the first one, my father signed to do six of them, if the first one made a certain number of credits. He never imagined that it would make any credits at all, but it blew past all expectations. He found himself having to make five more, even though he didn't want to."

"They're all excellent," Jeremy said. "Although the sixth has some flaws."

Laresta laughed. "My father was so fed up with the series by that time that he decided to kill off every single character. He was halfway through shooting the bloodbath when the storyline got leaked back to the owners of the property. They were furious. My father had to make a lot of changes very quickly. He didn't want to have to reshoot a single scene, so he edited everything he had together into a very different storyline."

Jeremy frowned. "That's not common knowledge."

"Nope. And I probably shouldn't be telling you, but I'm drunk," Laresta said.

"It certainly explains a lot," Jeremy said thoughtfully.

"She might not be telling the truth," Jonathan said.

Jeremy looked shocked. Then he nodded slowly. "She has had a lot to drink."

"It looks as if you both have," Jonathan said, waving a hand at the glasses on the table.

Jeremy flushed. "I think I've had too much. I need to go and lie down for a little while."

"No, don't go," Laresta said flatly.

The man flushed again. "I'll see you around," he said before he slowly stood up. He walked with exaggerated caution to the door. He reached for the button to open the door but missed. Seemingly unaware that he hadn't actually pressed the button, he took a step forward, walking right into the still-closed door.

"Ouch," he said as he bounced backward. He glanced around the room to see if anyone had noticed. From where I was sitting, it looked as if everyone in the room was watching him. He frowned and then reached for the button again. It took him three tries to actually hit it. While he'd been trying, he'd begun leaning on the door. Now it slid open, and he fell sideways out of the room. I heard several muffled curses as the door slid shut again.

"Oh dear," Laresta said.

Jonathan tapped on the table. A moment later, a bot flew over and began to remove all of the empty glasses.

"Do you want something to help you sober up?" he asked Laresta.

She shook her head. "I don't ever want to be sober again.

My father is dead. I can't even begin to imagine what I'm going to do next."

"You should inherit a great deal," Jonathan said.

Laresta wrinkled her nose. She tipped her head to one side and then shrugged. "This isn't about credits. My father taught me everything I know about the content creation business. And he managed my business for me. And he was my father. I don't want credits. I want my father back."

As she burst into tears, Jonathan tapped on the table. A glass of water and a box of tissues were delivered a few moments later. Laresta took a sip of water and then loudly blew her nose. Then she wiped her eyes.

"I'm sorry," she said. "I'm trying to deal with things, but I'm doing it badly."

"What did you have for lunch?" I asked her.

She looked confused by the question. "I don't think..."

"What do you want for lunch?" Jonathan asked, tapping to bring up the bar's menu on the table.

"I'm not hungry."

"But you need to eat. You need to keep your strength up," I said.

"I don't want to be strong," Laresta said.

"Soup," Jonathan said. "Tomato or chicken noodle?"

"Tomato."

"With garlic onion bread and some fruit for dessert," Jonathan said.

Laresta made a face. "I'd rather have something chocolate for dessert."

"You can have both."

Jonathan tapped in the order and then sat back in his seat. "It shouldn't take long."

"Thank you. I'm probably behaving badly. I probably need to stop drinking. I don't know what else to do."

"You can talk to me about the other people who were at the fire system test this morning," Jonathan said. "Maybe we can work out who had a reason to want to eliminate your father."

"That's an easy one. Zarina."

"Why?"

"My father was already growing tired of her. She's stupid and demanding and whiny and awful. I'm not sure what he ever saw in her, really."

"Did you get to meet her before they got married?" I asked.

"Yes, but after they got engaged, when it was really too late. My father was crazy about her and couldn't see who she truly was."

"She said they were planning to have a baby."

Laresta laughed. "Yeah, that was a lie. My father didn't want any more children. I was all that he needed or wanted. It didn't help that he'd had to raise me by himself after my mother left, of course."

"Did he do much of the work himself?" I blurted out.

She gave me an amused smile. "Of course not. I had nannies and tutors and paid playmates from the day I was born. I barely ever saw my father, but I always knew that he was there for me if I needed him."

"Tell me about the other people who were at the test this morning," Jonathan said.

"Why? None of them had any reason to want to kill my father. Zarina is the only one who stands to gain anything by his death."

"You're going to inherit a fortune," Jonathan said.

Laresta made a face. "But he was my father."

"Howard will have less competition," he suggested.

"My father wasn't really in competition with Howard,

not any longer. Howard was stuck on long-form production. My father had moved on to bigger and better things. Although they were actually smaller and better things, weren't they?"

A bot flew over to the table. It stopped and then carefully put a bowl of tomato soup on the table. Then it delivered a loaf of bread studded with garlic and covered in butter. The two desserts were on another plate together. After that was lowered into place, the bot flew away.

"I'm not hungry," Laresta said.

"Eat some soup," Jonathan told her. "I'll ask you a question after every spoonful."

She took a small bite of soup.

"I've been told that your father's rivalry with Howard was exaggerated for publicity purposes," Jonathan said. "Would you agree?"

"Oh, yeah. My father loved publicity. Any kind of publicity. And Howard is the same. He used to make nasty comments about my father's content, just to make headlines. Then my father would do the same back at him. That stopped when my father moved into immedieos, though. Howard made a few nasty comments about the format, but that was all he could do, really. My father stopped commenting on Howard's work at the same time."

"Did they discuss that and agree, or did it just happen?" Jonathan asked as she took a bigger mouthful.

"You'd have to ask Howard that. I've always thought that they were almost friends, really, behind their public rivalry, but I never once saw them together aside from a few very public meetings when they were nasty to one another."

"If they were actually friends, or at least friendly, is it possible that they recently had a falling-out?"

She sighed. "Anything is possible. I don't know how to

answer that question. I can't get my head around the idea that someone might have murdered my father. I keep telling myself that it must have been an accident. Murders happen on screen, not in my life." She looked at me. "They happen in your life, though. Maybe Jonathan should be asking you some difficult questions."

Jonathan shook his head. "I know Diana didn't have anything to do with your father's murder."

"I don't think Howard killed him. But I don't think anyone killed him. Unless it was Zarina. I can see her killing him. Except, I'm just saying that because I have to say something. I don't know what I'm saying."

"Eat your soup," I said. "Or have some bread. It smells wonderful."

Laresta stared at me blankly for a moment before tearing off a small amount of bread. She took a bite and then turned her attention back to Jonathan.

"This is a pointless conversation. I'm not thinking straight. I'm drunk."

"We can just talk about people," Jonathan said. "I'm curious about your relationship with the men and women who were at the test this morning."

"I don't have a relationship with most of them."

"What about Honey?"

"Who's Honey?"

"Honey Phillips. She's the woman whose shoulder you cried on after the body was found."

Laresta laughed. "I didn't even know her name. When the door opened and I saw my father, I just lost it. I started to sob. The two women who were with Howard sort of exchanged glances and then Honey pulled me into a hug. I never asked her for her name or anything. I just cried until I couldn't cry any longer. And then I went and talked to Shawn and the security bot for what felt like hours."

"So let's talk about the people you do know," Jonathan said as Laresta took another bite of bread. "I understand you've met Craig Martelle on a few occasions."

She wrinkled her nose again. "I love military men. They're so serious all the time. And strong and brave and handsome. I mean, they can't all be handsome, can they? But I've never met a member of Space Corps who wasn't handsome."

"It's one of the requirements," Jonathan said with a perfectly straight face.

Laresta stared at him. "Will you admit that on an immedieo? That's a soundblip that could make us both millions."

Jonathan chuckled. "I was just teasing."

"Were you, though?" Laresta asked.

"Tell me about Craig."

"I don't know what to tell you. He's handsome and brave and just a little bit scary. You're even scarier, though. Except you seem incredibly nice, so maybe I'm not as scared of you as I am of Craig."

"He told me that he got you off Splestra."

She nodded. "I was too young and stupid to be scared, even when we were told that the planet was probably going to explode. We were all young and rich and we all felt invincible."

"And then the planet exploded," Jonathan said.

"Yeah, but by that time we were all safely on a totally amazing Space Corps ship full of handsome men and beautiful women in those fancy Space Corps uniforms."

"I lost a good friend when Splestra blew," Jonathan said.

Laresta looked at me. "See what I mean? They're always so serious." She looked at Jonathan. "I'm sorry about your friend. I really am. I'm also sorry that I was dumb enough to ignore the early warnings and that Space Corps had to send a team in to drag me and my friends off the planet. I told Captain Martelle as much the last time I saw him. Well, the last time before today, that is."

Jonathan nodded. "Can you think of any reason why he might have wanted your father dead?"

She stared at him for a moment before laughing. "No, not at all. And if he did decide to kill someone, he would probably just shoot them and walk away. I can't see him doing anything as elaborate and tricky as what happened to my father. Or maybe I'm just dumb, and killing my father was super easy. Whatever, I can't imagine Craig being behind it."

"What about Tammy?"

"Oh, goodness, no," she exclaimed. "Tammy is an icon among women. She founded her own planet. And it's a very successful planet, too. Did you know that seventy-two percent of newly-founded planets fail within the first five years? Tammy knew that, but she didn't let it stop her."

"She knew your father."

"She dated my father for a while. We talked a few times. I liked her better than most of the women my father dated. Then my father met Zarina, and he stopped thinking."

Jonathan nodded. "What about Becca?"

"She's so kind. I'd never met her before today, but she took charge when my father was found, and then she came to see me to make sure I was okay. She even gave me something and told me to get some sleep."

"But you came here instead," Jonathan said.

"I felt so alone. I couldn't stay in my suite, not all alone."

"What about Iris, the Nadoian?"

"I've never seen one in person before my father introduced me to her a few days ago. Of course I'd seen the documentary my father made about them, but I watched it years ago. I suppose I wasn't even sure that Nadoians were real."

"She and your father remained friends after he finished the documentary," Jonathan said.

"My father had a lot of friends. He didn't introduce me to many of them. That was changing as I got older, but he was still quite particular about who I met. In some ways, he could be a bit controlling."

"Did that bother you?" I asked.

She pushed her half-empty soup bowl away and picked up a fork. Then she stabbed a piece of chocolate cake. After she'd chewed and swallowed it, she looked at me.

"Maybe. Which isn't a proper answer, but I'm not sure how to answer, really. I never gave it much thought, but I should have thought about it. When I did think too much, though, I got really sad. I've always been very aware that my life would have been very different if my mother had stayed. Sometimes I think I miss her more now than I did when I was a child."

"How well do you know Captain Ryder?" Jonathan asked after an awkward silence.

She shrugged. "He's the ship's captain. He took us on a tour of the entire ship when we were still in Alpha Sector. He comes in here most evenings. We've talked, but never about anything important. His uniform is almost as handsome as a Space Corps uniform, but he doesn't flirt no matter how hard I try."

"He could get fired for doing so," Jonathan said.

"Well, that's just dumb."

"What about Troy?"

"Troy?"

"Troy Dyffryn, the photographer."

"I didn't know his name. And I won't remember it. But what about him?"

"He did a photo shoot with you years ago."

"He did? If you say so. I've done a lot of shoots over the years. I don't remember any of the photographers, even though some of them have been quite famous."

"Troy used to be quite famous for photographing weddings," I said.

She shrugged. "I haven't made that mistake yet."

"So you don't remember Troy at all?" Jonathan asked.

"Not even a little bit. Why? Do you think it's possible that he had something to do with my father's death?"

Jonathan shook his head. "I think your father's death was very personal."

Laresta inhaled slowly. "I don't know what to say to that."

"You should eat and then get some rest," Jonathan said.

"What are you going to do?" she asked.

"Everything I can to find your father's killer."

She took another bite of cake and chewed very slowly. "It might have been an accident," she said after she'd swallowed.

"Maybe."

"Or not. Is he always this serious?" she asked me.

I nodded. "Pretty much."

"I need sleep," Laresta said. "I'm so tired."

"We'll walk you back to your suite," Jonathan said.

"I can manage on my own. I need to get used to the idea of doing things on my own. I relied far too much on my father." She stood up and took a few steps toward the door. "I can do this," she said before she stumbled her way to the door.

She managed to hit the button to open the door on her first try. I watched as she walked through it and then turned left.

"That poor girl," I said.

"Save your sympathy until we find the killer."

I stared at Jonathan.

TEN

"Do you really think that she killed her own father?" I asked.

He shrugged. "I don't think anything yet. We have a lot more people we need to talk to before we get to that point."

I sighed. "So what's next?"

"I'm going to message a few people. Hopefully they'll all be willing to talk to me."

"You haven't asked anyone about Shawn or Jerry," I said when Jonathan finally put his comms away.

"And I should be asking for the sake of completeness. We both know that Shawn couldn't hack his own systems if his life depended on it, though."

"Jerry could hack the entire ship. Maybe he already has."

Jonathan nodded. "But if he wanted to get rid of someone, he'd do so in a way that he'd never get caught. I suspect if he killed someone, the body would never be found."

I shivered. "Okay. Let's not talk about Shawn or Jerry."

He chuckled. "Let's go and talk to Becca. She made room in her schedule for us."

"That was kind of her."

"She's a kind person."

"Everyone seems to love her."

"Yes, which is slightly worrying. Some of the galaxy's most successful serial killers were incredibly nice people."

"Aside from the murders, you mean."

"Yeah, aside from that."

We walked out of the bar and then down the corridor to the medical unit. Jonathan pressed the door's buzzer. The door slid open a moment later. We walked into the suite's small waiting room. A medical bot was bobbing in place in the center of the room.

"What is your emergency?" it asked.

"No emergency. We're here to see Becca," Jonathan replied.

"I can scan you and administer all necessary aid. We do not need to disturb the Chief Medical Officer," the bot said.

"Oh, go away," Linda said as she walked into the room. "You'd think it was being paid by the patient or something," she said to us. "She tries to convince everyone who comes in here that they don't need to see Becca, that she can take care of them."

"Can she, er, it?" I asked.

"I really must stop calling it 'she,' but I do prefer to think of it as a female bot, even though I know bots don't actually have genders. Where was I? Can it actually help? It can bandage up cuts, if they're obviously bleeding. It can also spray minor burns with an appropriate ointment. Just about anything more serious needs me or Becca. Mostly Becca, because I'm still working thorough my medical training."

"I can treat more than a hundred and seventy-six

different illnesses and other medical needs," the bot said. "And I'm getting smarter every day."

"That's right, I forgot. It can diagnose a few different bugs and provide the correct treatment for them. Except one of the good things about long-distance space travel is that if no one boards the ship with a cold or a fever, we should all be safe from them during our journey."

"Except we're making several planetary stops," I said.

She nodded. "There is that. But if someone does bring a virus back to the ship, we can spray antivirals into every cabin while everyone is asleep and take care of it within minutes."

"Can they do that?" I asked Jonathan.

"It was in the fine print when you bought your ticket," Linda said. "The crew can do just about anything they feel is necessary to keep the passengers safe and well during their journey."

I nodded. "I really should have read the fine print."

Jonathan laughed. "No one reads the fine print. The big corporations rely on that. That's how over a thousand children got named AntiBanGo all those years ago."

Linda nodded. "I read about that."

I nodded. "I read about it, too, but I still don't read the fine print, even knowing that some junior employee put a clause in his company's fine print stating that anyone who used their product had to name their next child 'AntiBanGo' after the product."

"The employee had been given the job of putting together all of the warnings and instructions for the product and he thought it would be funny to insert that clause. He also expected someone to proofread what he'd put together. Unfortunately for him and the company, even his supervisors didn't want to read the fine print. Once the product launched, someone did read it all, though, and she made headlines when she named her newborn son AntiBanGo," Jonathan said.

"And then she threatened to sue the company if they didn't enforce that clause and force all of their customers to do the same," Linda said. "In the end, only a small percentage of people who'd bought the product actually named their children AntiBanGo, mostly people living on Ruesurn."

"Because they have a strong culture of rule-following on Ruesurn," Jonathan said. "The company immediately took the clause out and declared that it was null and void and that no one needed to worry about it, but that raised a lot of issues with the very nature of what's included in those kinds of documents. For a while it looked as if some proper changes might get made to how those documents were written. Then something else happened somewhere else in the galaxy and everyone lost interest in changing anything."

"And a thousand kids grew up with that unfortunate name," I said.

"Most of them changed their names as soon as they were legally able," Linda said. "I saw a documentary about them once. Only a handful lived with that name for their entire lives. One of those who did was the very first one to be given the name. He saw it as a badge of honor or something. And he also got a ton of credits from AntiBanGo as a sort of apology."

Jonathan chuckled. "We came to see Becca," he said.

Linda nodded. "She knows that you're here. She's in the middle of something, though. She'll be out soon."

"I'm here," Becca said as she rushed into the room.

"How are you?" Jonathan asked.

She shrugged. "Busy. Autopsies take a lot of time, especially when murder is suspected."

"It seems quite obvious that it was murder, considering the man was drugged and then left in a space where the oxygen was then removed," Jonathan said.

"No comment," Becca said.

Jonathan grinned. "As I understand it, Carl died at least an hour before the fire-control systems test began. That makes it even more apparent that he was murdered."

"No comment," Becca said.

"How many of the people who were at the test do you know?" Jonathan asked.

She shrugged. "I do my best to meet all of the passengers on any ship where I'm assigned. I believe I'd met everyone who was there this morning. I wouldn't say that I know any of them well, though."

"You know Captain Ryder well," Jonathan said. "And Shawn and Jerry and Troy."

Becca made a face. "I wasn't including crew in my comment. I do know Captain Ryder. We've worked together on a number of occasions. He's a talented captain and a good man. He didn't have anything to do with Carl's death. As for Shawn, I can't see him being involved, either. If Jerry had done it, he would have, at the very least, locked that bathroom door so that no one accidentally discovered the body. And then, after the test was complete, he would have jettisoned the body into space."

"And Troy?" Jonathan asked.

"Troy is still recovering from his injuries. I don't think he's up to planning and executing a murder right now. Of course, knowing Troy, I can't imagine him ever planning and executing a murder for any number of reasons."

"You knew the victim?"

"In passing. I met him and his wife and his daughter when Captain Ryder took them on a tour of the ship. I suggested that he come in for regular scans when I met him. He nodded and ignored me like most people do."

"What about Howard?"

"Again, he was given a tour of the ship that included the medical unit. He came around with Honey and Ava. Ava is the only one that I ever saw again."

"Oh?"

She shook her head. "She consulted me about her health. Everything in that regard is confidential."

Jonathan nodded. "What about Craig and Tammy Martelle?"

"I met Craig years ago when I did a short stint on a Space Corps ship. We've maybe exchanged ten words in total since that day. I've never actually met Tammy, although I saw her this morning."

"What about Iris?"

"She's probably the person I know best out of the passengers who were at the test this morning."

"Really? She only joined the ship recently."

Becca nodded. "But as soon as she came aboard, I reached out to her. I've been working on learning Nado for decades following online tutorials. I was hoping she might be willing to provide some in-person tutoring."

"And was she?"

"Yes. She's been incredibly generous with her time, really. We work together every other day for an hour at a time."

"Is it helping?"

"Oh, goodness, yes. The difference between working with a real person versus working online is night and day. There are so many incredibly subtle variations in movements that make the language rich and complex and it's nearly impossible to recognize them when watching a tutorial or working with a language-tutoring bot. I'm sure my skills have improved a hundredfold since I started working with Iris. I'm excited to see how far I can get before we arrive in Val Segas."

"Do you think it's possible that Iris murdered Carl?" Jonathan asked.

Becca shook her head. "She and Carl were friends. We talked about their friendship. She cared very deeply for the man. I know that she's very upset about his untimely death."

"Is there anything else you can tell us about Carl's murder or the people who were at the test this morning?" Jonathan asked.

"I'm sorry, but I don't think there is," Becca said. "If I were you, though, I'd take a good look at the ship's logs for C Deck. The killer had to have hacked quite a few things in order to accomplish what he or she managed."

Jonathan nodded. "Got it. Thank you."

We got up and headed for the door.

"Thanks," I said to Linda.

She nodded. "It was good to see you again," she said.

In the corridor, Jonathan looked at me. "We need to find what Becca found," he said. "I already have my computer looking through all of the logs for the ship, but I'm going to start another search, specific to C Deck and within a very narrow time window, starting about an hour before the test started."

I leaned against the wall while Jonathan tapped away on his comms. Even though I was learning programming, I had no idea how he was structuring his requests to the system. Searching logs that might have been tampered with was way beyond my computer skills. He was still working when someone turned the corner and started walking toward us.

"Good afternoon," I said to Troy as he approached.

He frowned. "I wasn't expecting to see you here."

"We were just talking to Becca," I said.

"I need to see her. I'm still getting treatments on a few of my injuries," he said, gesturing toward a scar on his forehead. "She's doing what she can to speed up the healing process."

"Let's talk," Jonathan said as he looked up from his comms. "Do you want to get your treatment first?"

Troy glanced at his wrist unit and shrugged. "I'm early. We can talk before my treatment. I don't have anything to tell you, though. I don't know anything about the murder this morning."

"Let's go and sit somewhere comfortable," Jonathan suggested.

We walked the short distance to one of the lounges and walked inside. Several couches were slowly floating their way around the room. There wasn't anyone there. Jonathan tapped on his comms. A couch settled on the floor in front of us. As soon as we were all sitting comfortably, it lifted and then began to move in a lazy circuit of the room.

"These things make me queasy," Troy said.

"I can make it stationary," Jonathan said.

Troy shook his head. "If it keeps moving, I'll have more incentive to talk faster."

"Tell me about the people who were at the test this morning."

Troy stared at him. "Tell you about them? I don't know any of them – not really, anyway. I mean, I know Becca. She was there. She saved my life. If you want to know if I think she killed Carl Seintruber, then no, I don't.

If Becca wanted to kill someone, she's smart enough to find a way to do it so that it would look like natural causes. And she's the Chief Medical Officer on the ship. If she did kill someone, she could falsify the autopsy results anyway."

"What about Captain Ryder?"

"He's too busy running the ship to worry about any of the individual passengers. And if he did kill someone, he could order Becca to falsify her reports. But before he did that, he'd probably just dump the body into space."

"What about Shawn?"

Troy looked around the room and then leaned close to Jonathan. "He's too stupid to get away with murder. If he'd done it, he'd have dropped his wallet in the man's lap or something. But he would never actually kill anyone himself, anyway. He's never done anything himself. That's why he has an assistant who goes everywhere with him. If Shawn wanted someone dead, he'd tell Jerry and Jerry would make that person disappear without a trace."

"So you don't think any of the crew had anything to do with the man's death," Jonathan concluded.

"I guess not."

"What about Carl's wife or daughter?"

"They both make content for a living. As far as I know, they're both very successful. I haven't had many opportunities to take their pictures because they're in suites, which means they don't usually go to the dining room or other public places. I have taken pictures in the private bar once or twice, but Captain Ryder always throws me out as soon as he gets a single complaint about me."

"You did a photo shoot for Laresta on Val Segas," Jonathan said.

"Yeah. I did photo shoots for thousands of people on Val

Segas. I barely remember her, and I don't remember anything about the shoot."

"What about Howard or Honey or Ava?"

Troy shook his head. "This is a waste of time. I don't know them. I don't know anything about them. I'm just here to take pictures."

"What about Craig Martelle?"

"He doesn't like me. I don't think he likes anyone. But he's former Space Corps. He's too smart to murder someone on the ship. If he'd wanted Carl dead, he'd have gotten him alone on Caboluxous and then left the body there."

"And Tammy?"

Troy smiled. "Tammy is one of the most amazing women in the world. Our paths crossed occasionally when I was still shooting weddings on Val Segas. She always made a point to speak to me kindly. I refuse to believe that she had anything to do with Carl's death."

"What about Iris JaKay?"

Troy sighed. "Nadoians are almost impossible to photograph well. So much of how they express themselves is through their hands. They never know how to smile properly for a camera, not unless they can use their hands to express their feelings at the same time. But moving hands are a distraction in a still photograph."

"Do you know Iris?" Jonathan asked.

"She travels a great deal as a reporter for her planet. We'd met a few times over the years. I only ever agreed to photograph one Nadoian wedding. Iris was the guest of honor at the ceremony and the reception. Those were some of the very worst photos I've ever taken in my career."

"Do you think it's possible that she killed Carl?"

He shook his head. "She and Carl were friends. I think

she was the most upset person in the room when his body was found."

"So who do you think killed Carl?" Jonathan asked.

"It wasn't an accident? I mean, maybe he just fell asleep in the bathroom and didn't wake up when the oxygen was sucked out."

Jonathan shook his head. "It wasn't an accident."

Troy looked thoughtful. "I don't know any of the suspects well enough to have a proper opinion, but if I were you, I'd look closely at Howard. He and Carl were rivals. Rumor has it that Howard was planning a move into immedieos. They're quick and cheap to make and they can generate a ton of income very quickly. I'm surprised everyone in the content business isn't making them, really."

"Interesting. Thank you," Jonathan said. "Why did you decide to open the door to the bathroom?" he asked.

Troy flushed. "I just wanted to get a picture of it," he said.

"Why?"

"I just want to document everything on the ship."

Jonathan frowned. "I'm sure that InmonCorp was very exact in their measurements. The cabin and its bathroom will meet intergalactic standards."

"Maybe on paper, but it certainly didn't feel like enough space for two people on a long-distance space journey. And it's supposed to be a cabin for two. I checked."

"Still chasing news headlines, even after everything that's happened to you?" Jonathan asked.

Troy shrugged. "I was thinking more of an exposé on InmonCorp." He looked around the room and then sighed. "I shouldn't have said that out loud."

Jonathan nodded. He tapped on the couch's arm. It slowly floated to the ground. I jumped up quickly, not trusting it to stay in place for long. Troy and Jonathan moved more slowly. As soon as they were both standing, the couch shot up six feet into the air and then quickly glided away.

"I'd better get to the medical wing," Troy said.

"Before you rush off, I want copies of all of the pictures that you took this morning," Jonathan said.

"They've all been uploaded to the system. I can send them to you, or you can just hack your way into the system and get them."

"I try to keep my hacking to a minimum," Jonathan said with a thin smile. "Please send them to me."

"Now?"

"As soon as possible."

Troy sighed. "I'll do it now, before I forget."

He pulled out his comms and scrolled through several screens. "Do you want everything from the entire day or just the pictures I took on C Deck?"

"Give me the entire day. Sometimes unexpected things can be helpful."

"Sent."

"Thank you."

Troy looked at his wrist unit and frowned. "I'm going to be late," he said as he rushed toward the door.

Jonathan and I followed more slowly.

"Now what?" I asked Jonathan as we walked into the corridor.

"Now we're going to have a little chat with Iris."

ELEVEN

As he started to walk away, I rushed to keep up with him.

"Are you sure you want me to come along?" I asked. "I don't seem to be doing anything besides sitting there and listening."

"That's what I'm counting on, that you're listening."

I thought about arguing, but I was too interested in spending time with an actual Nadoian to do so. We walked back to the corridor with the suites. Jonathan knocked on a door. When it opened, Iris smiled at us both.

"Welcome," she said, her hands moving through a series of gestures.

"Thank you," Jonathan said. He raised his hands and executed a clumsy sign.

Iris chuckled. "I don't think you meant that," she said.

"What did I say?"

"You said 'It's nearly time for the creatures who dance in the toast.'"

Jonathan frowned. "I thought that was just 'hello' and 'thank you.'"

"This is hello," Iris said, moving her hands in a simple sign that I remembered from my brief study.

"That's a medium formal hello, mostly used between acquaintances who are not yet friends. There are other versions depending on how well you know the person or persons you are greeting. Thank you is more complex. There are degrees of thankfulness to consider as well as the relationship between yourself and the other person. There are special ways to express thanks for gifts as opposed to other kindnesses."

Jonathan held up a hand. "Never mind. Hello. And thanks for agreeing to talk to us."

She nodded. "Please come in."

The words were accompanied by a simple sign that somehow made me feel more welcome. We walked into the suite, which was nearly identical to Jonathan's.

"Please sit," Iris said.

She waved us toward the couches. I walked over and sat down. Jonathan sat next to me.

"I'm going to apologize in advance," Iris said. "I have spent most of this afternoon in floods of tears." Her hands and arms seemed to move with heavy sadness as she spoke. "I lost a dear friend this morning."

"I'm sorry to have to ask you about him and his death," Jonathan said.

She shook her head. "I want to talk about him. I want to do everything I can to help you find the person who ended his life. It's simply going to be difficult for me to share my memories of Carl. He was an incredible person who enriched my life in many ways."

"Tell us about him," Jonathan said.

"What do you want to know?"

Jonathan shrugged. "We've been talking to people about

who might have murdered him, but I don't feel as if we know much about him as a person. Tell us about the man you befriended thirty years ago."

She nodded. Her eyes got a faraway look, and her hands began to move in a graceful pattern that seemed to repeat itself as she spoke. "We worked together on his project. I was happy to help. Even before I met him, I was interested in helping. I wanted to make sure that the story that he told was accurate. There are a lot of misconceptions about my people in the galaxy."

Jonathan nodded. "Carl's documentary did something to help address that."

"It did. It was a joy to be a part of it. And it was a joy to become Carl's friend. At the time, I rather assumed that once he'd finished the story, I'd never see or speak to him again, but after he left, he stayed in touch. And when we were both traveling and happened to be in the same part of the galaxy at the same time, he always tried to find time to see me."

"Was the relationship ever romantic?" Jonathan asked.

She flushed and then slowly shook her head. "I was never interested in him in a romantic way. When we first met, he suggested that we might explore something in that way, but he was very polite when I refused."

I watched her hands flutter anxiously back and forth as she spoke.

"We were friends. We became close friends. But we were never lovers," she said firmly.

"Tell us about his first marriage," I said.

Jonathan looked amused by my question.

"Natalie," Iris said flatly. She folded her hands in her lap. "We only met once," she said. "She didn't care for me."

"Was she jealous of the relationship that you had with Carl?" I asked.

"Maybe. Probably. I understand that she wanted Carl to travel less and spend more time at home with her. But I don't believe that she properly understood Carl's business. There was no way that he could stay in one place for months on end. He needed to travel in order to do his work." Her hands fluttered again.

"And then they had a baby," I said.

Iris sighed, dropping her hands into her lap again. "Carl wanted children. That was one of the reasons why he married Natalie. We talked, just after his marriage, before I'd had a chance to meet Natalie. He told me that they were planning to have a dozen children."

"A dozen?" I echoed.

"Carl loved Natalie. He loved people. His own upbringing had been rather empty and lonely. He was an only child. His mother was an actress, and his father was a set designer. They dragged Carl all over the galaxy, wherever they could find work. Carl wanted something different for his children. He wanted them to grow up in a large family with a mother who was actively involved in their lives."

"Things didn't go at all the way he'd planned, then," I said.

Iris's hands signed for several seconds before she spoke again. "Natalie agreed to all of that before they got married. She made him a number of promises about how their married life would be. And then, once they were actually married, she told him that she'd changed her mind about almost everything."

"But they stayed together, at least for a while," I said.

"Natalie agreed to a single child. She said she might

agree to more after the first, but she wanted to see what being a mother was actually like before she committed herself to future children. Carl had wanted her to carry the baby herself, but she flatly refused to do that. When they went to have the baby created, she only consented to the creation of a single embryo. Doctors usually prefer to create several and then choose the strongest for incubation. That also gives a couple the chance to have additional children in the future without having to go through the entire process a second time."

"She was determined to have only one child," Jonathan said.

Iris nodded. "She knew that if they created multiple embryos that Carl could choose to have additional children later, even if she and Carl were no longer together."

"I thought both parents had to agree to the incubation of embryos," I said.

"There are exceptions," Iris said. "Carl had enough credits to pay for an exception. The doctors wouldn't have had to worry about any child of his ever wanting for anything."

"Except a mother's love," I said.

"Carl did his best to provide Laresta with love," Iris said. Her hands moved slowly back and forth. "He adored his child. He visited her in her incubation chamber at least once a month even though he spent most of her gestation on the other side of the galaxy from the lab where she was developing. He talked to her and interacted with her chamber. Natalie visited exactly once. Carl said that he was told that she stayed for less than ten minutes."

"She didn't really want children," I said.

"I suspect you're correct," Iris said. "But she'd knowingly married a man who did want children. If she didn't want them, she never should have married Carl."

"What happened after the baby arrived?" Jonathan asked.

"Natalie and Carl were both there when the chamber was opened, and the baby emerged. Carl held her first, though. Carl told me later that Natalie seemed somewhat disgusted by the blood and goo that covered the newborn. She waited until the medical team cleaned the baby up and put some clothes on her before she held her."

"How long after that did Natalie leave?" I asked.

"Days. Maybe weeks. It might have been longer. I'm not certain. Carl didn't like to talk about it, and I never pushed him on the topic." Her hands rested for a moment before she continued. "Carl hired several nannies and other caretakers for Laresta. Natalie didn't have to lift a finger to help, but Carl did want her to spend time with the baby every day. He told me later that she spent less than an hour with Laresta each day, preferring to continue living her life as if the baby had never been born."

"Motherhood doesn't come naturally to all women," Jonathan said.

Iris nodded. "After a time, Natalie went to Carl and told him that she wanted to leave. She said that being a mother wasn't for her. Of course, she knew that Carl wanted the baby desperately and that he'd take good care of Laresta once she was gone. Carl offered her a large number of credits in exchange for full custody of Laresta. Natalie left the next day. She told him that she was going to settle on the desert planet of Florzonia and enjoy never having to work again thanks to him."

"Is she still there?" I asked.

Iris looked surprised by the question, her hands flying in

opposite directions as she stared at me. "I don't know," she said eventually.

"Would you recognize her if she were on the *Lady Elizabeth?*" I asked.

Iris sat back and closed her eyes. She put her hands on her lap and took several deep breaths. When she sat back up, her hands moved slowly as she spoke.

"I don't know. I met her only once. We barely spoke at that meeting. That was over twenty years ago. I remember very little about her. And it's possible that she has made changes to her appearance over the years. And she's grown older, of course. Often, when I meet people, it is their voice that I remember, rather than their face. She said not much more than a dozen words to me. I can't recall anything about her voice."

"Was she very upset with Carl when she left?" I asked.

Iris frowned. "Not at all. None of what happened was Carl's fault. She knew that he wanted children. She discovered that she did not. In my opinion, Carl was very generous to her with his settlement. I've always thought that he should have given her nothing but a divorce. He was still in love with her, though."

"Do you think he would have recognized her if she'd turned up on the ship?" I asked.

"They were together for two years. They were married and had a child together. I would expect that he'd recognize her, even if she'd altered her appearance, but I could be wrong about that."

"Is it possible that one of the women at the test this morning was Natalie?" I asked.

Again, Iris's hands moved in opposite directions, indicating her surprise. "The women this morning..." she said slowly. "But I was there. I didn't recognize anyone."

"This is Diana's pet theory," Jonathan said.

I bristled at his tone. It sounded patronizing to me.

"Never mind," I said.

Iris shook her head. "But it might matter. Obviously, Tammy Martelle isn't Natalie. She was rather busy elsewhere in the years that Natalie was with Carl."

"That leaves Honey, Ava, and Becca," I said.

"Natalie would never have managed to study medicine and work her way up to Chief Medical Officer on a ship like this. I believe Becca is probably too young anyway," Iris said. "The other two women, though, Honey Phillips and Ava Ross, they might be around the right age."

I nodded. "Could one of them be Natalie?"

"I don't know," Iris said. "I didn't speak to either of them this morning. And I don't recall hearing either of them speak. Neither of them look the way I remember Natalie looking, but she's had decades to make changes to her appearance. Voices are harder to change. If you could arrange for me to hear both of their voices, I might be able to identify one of them as Natalie, at least tentatively."

"We're working on locating Natalie now," Jonathan said. "We've no reason to believe that she's anywhere other than on Florzonia."

"I almost want to believe that one of them is Natalie," Iris said, her hands soaring upwards. "It would be a great relief to me if one of them killed Carl."

"A relief? Why?" Jonathan asked.

"I have been pacing back and forth for hours, trying to work out who killed Carl. I kept coming back to the two people who were closest to him. And I hate the idea that he was killed by his wife or his daughter. Either would be horrible, but the idea that Laresta might have killed him is far worse."

"Do you think she might have?"

"I don't know. I don't know her at all, even though Carl often spoke to me about her. I will say that over the years Carl's words built a picture of her in my mind. When I met her for the first time, I was struck by how little she resembled that picture."

"What was different?" I asked.

"Nothing and everything. Of course Carl always told me only the best things about his daughter. I suppose I didn't realize how much that had colored my ideas about her. I was expecting her to be smart and kind and devoted to Carl. Instead, she's clever, scheming, and from what I saw, she was more interested in manipulating Carl than in caring about him."

"She's still very young," Jonathan said.

"I can't imagine that she'll improve with age," Iris said dryly, her hands moving very slowly.

"Is she at the top of your suspect list?" I asked.

"She and Zarina were together in the top spot," Iris said. "But now I'm rethinking everything I spent the afternoon thinking."

"Don't get too hung up on Diana's theory," Jonathan said.

"It does seem remotely possible," Iris said. "And I very much prefer it to any of the other options."

"Even if Natalie is on the ship, that doesn't mean she killed Carl," Jonathan said.

"But it makes sense. Maybe she ran out of credits and tried to hit him up for more. Or maybe she decided that she now wanted to be a part of her daughter's life, but Carl refused to let her see Laresta. There are many possibilities."

"Laresta is an adult. Carl couldn't stop Natalie from seeing her," I said.

"Except I believe he controlled Laresta's life. That sounds quite bad. What I mean is that he was not only her father, but also her employer. They traveled everywhere together, and I believe her father handled all of her appointments on her behalf."

"Considering her line of work, he could have argued that doing so was for her own good," Jonathan said.

Iris nodded. "There are a lot of stalkers out there who latch on to content creators. I know a woman who let one get too close and nearly got herself killed in the process. Carl was simply being careful."

"Does he do the same for Zarina?" I asked.

Iris's hands fluttered. "You'd have to ask Zarina about that. She was already an adult with her own life when she and Carl met. He might have trusted her to take care of herself. Or maybe she was happy to turn over that responsibility to Carl after they were married. The attention that some content creators can get can be overwhelming for many of them."

"Can you think of any reason why anyone else might have wanted to get rid of Carl?" Jonathan asked.

"Earlier, before we talked, I was worried about Howard."

"Do you know him?"

She nodded. "Not well, but we've met. Not long after I worked with Carl, Howard came to Nado. He wanted to do something similar to Carl's documentary, but more sensational. I refused to work with him and urged the Nadoian Council to refuse him permission to shoot on our planet. He offered the Council a huge number of credits, far more than Carl had paid, but the Council listened to me and told him no. He ended up making a low-budget short docudrama that he claimed was set on Nado but was actually shot somewhere else. It flopped, at least in part because none of the actors were actually Nadoians. They simply talked back and forth while waving their arms around."

"I saw it," I said. "I was trying to learn a bit of Nado at the time, and I found it really confusing because nothing they were doing made any sense."

"They made no effort at all to learn the language. They simply pretended to use it," Iris said, her gestures expressing her sadness.

"So you aren't a fan of Howard Howard," Jonathan said.

"Actually, I'm a huge fan of some of his work," she said. "He's done some incredibly brilliant things over the decades he's been working. I just don't respect him as a person."

"Does he know that?" I asked.

She shrugged. "We've never spoken, not since that single conversation thirty years ago. Until this morning, I was unaware that he was on the ship."

"And you don't know either of the women with him?" Jonathan asked.

"Not unless one of them is Natalie," Iris said. "I've seen a few of Honey's stories. She's a very talented storyteller. Knowing Howard, Ava is also very talented. He surrounds himself with people who are smarter than he is."

"Clever people often do," Jonathan said.

"So do some stupid people, although that's more luck than judgment," Iris said.

"It's easier for stupid people. Just about everyone they meet qualifies," I suggested.

They both laughed, Iris's hands fluttered back and forth, fingers waving individually as her hands moved.

"So you think we should take a closer look at Howard," Jonathan said.

"I know nothing about spaceships or computers. I can

manage to transmit my reports back to Nado and very little else. But I have to believe that whoever killed Carl did some hacking in order to get everything into place. Howard has excellent computer skills. He needs them in order to do his job. Carl was the same, but, of course, Carl didn't kill himself."

"It certainly seems unlikely that he killed himself," Jonathan said.

"He would never have done such a thing," Iris said. "His mother killed herself when he was in his early twenties. Her death had a profound effect on him. We talked about it a great deal. No matter what happened to him in life, he would never have put Laresta through what he endured."

"I don't think that Becca is seriously considering suicide as a cause of death, but that's still good to know," Jonathan said.

Iris frowned. "I'm exhausted. I'm very sorry, but is it possible for us to be finished? I think I need some rest."

"We're finished," Jonathan said. "Thank you very much for your time."

"Thank you," I said as I got to my feet.

"I wish you both the very best of luck in finding the person who did this," Iris said as she walked with us to the door. "I know I won't be able to sleep properly until he or she has been found."

"We're doing all that we can," Jonathan said. He tapped the button to open the door.

"Thanks again," I said as I followed Jonathan into the hall.

Iris nodded. She didn't speak, but her hands were still moving as the door slid shut.

I leaned against the wall. "I'm tired, too," I said.

"It's getting late. You need some dinner."

"Dinner? We just had lunch." I glanced at my wrist unit. "Six hours ago?" I said questioningly.

"I think we both need a break for tonight. We can start again in the morning."

"Start where?"

"We're having breakfast with Howard, Honey, and Ava."

"We are?"

He nodded. "Why don't you go back to your cabin and have some dinner delivered. Meet me at my cabin at nine."

I nodded. "I can do that," I said before yawning.

"The adrenaline from the morning is wearing off. You're about to crash," he told me.

He walked me to my door. "Good night," he said.

"Good night," I replied, yawning again as my door opened. I walked into my cabin and then waved at Jonathan as the door slid shut.

TWELVE

I was halfway through getting Singer her breakfast the next morning when an alarm started.

"There is a fire on B Deck. Please stand by for further instructions," the mechanical voice said.

"I'm not on B Deck," I muttered. "We should be just fine," I told Singer as I finished filling her food bowl.

"Meewww," she replied, not obviously bothered by the loud beeping noise that seemed to fill my cabin.

I checked that Singer had everything she needed and then grabbed my bag and headed for the door.

When I tapped, the door didn't open. I tapped again.

"There is a fire on B Deck. All passengers are asked to remain in their cabins until the fire is under control," a voice told me.

"I'm not on B Deck," I said loudly.

"The fire has been contained," a different voice said. "Thank you all for your patience during this emergency."

"I wasn't patient," I said as I pushed the button for the door again.

It slid open. I walked out into the corridor and then shut

the door behind me. Jonathan's suite was only a short distance away.

"Another fire?" I asked him when he opened his door to my knock.

"One of the smart young passengers on B Deck decided that this morning would be a good time to test the ship's fire-control system."

"After Carl's death, I don't think I'd be testing anything today."

"Carl's death hasn't been announced to the general population yet. I suspect everyone on A Deck is aware of what happened, but I'm not sure that knowledge has spread to B Deck yet."

"Craig is on B Deck."

"But Craig doesn't speak to people unless he has to."

I laughed. "Fair enough. But what did the guy on B Deck do to test the system?"

"He put a small pile of dirty laundry on his bed and then set it on fire."

I frowned. "That's just crazy."

"Indeed. Luckily for everyone, the fire-control system worked pretty well for him. A fire-control bot was dispatched. It managed to stop the fire from spreading, but didn't have enough foam onboard to completely extinguish it. Instead, it triggered the cabin's sprinkler system. Everything in the cabin got covered in foam, but the fire was put out reasonably quickly."

I shook my head. "What's going to happen to the guy who started the fire?"

"He's being moved into a cabin on C Deck while his cabin is drying out."

I made a face. "That seems like a harsh punishment."

"There aren't any cabins available on B Deck right now.

And Captain Ryder didn't dare move him to A Deck. Every other passenger on B Deck would have started a fire within an hour if it got out that a fire in your cabin got you a cabin on A Deck."

I nodded. "Should we be happy that there hasn't been a rush of people finding dead bodies to get onto A Deck?"

"Definitely. Don't think that some of the passengers on B Deck haven't thought about it. If we weren't so good at finding the killers, someone might have tried something by now."

"Are we still having breakfast with Howard, Honey, and Ava?"

"We are. Are you ready?"

"I suppose so. I'm feeling oddly disoriented by the fire alarm, though. Maybe just because of everything that happened yesterday."

"Let's go," Jonathan said.

We walked a short distance and stopped in front of an unmarked door. Jonathan tapped on the panel next to it. He scanned his comms and then typed in a code. The door slid open.

"What is this?" I asked as we walked into a small room. There was a table with six chairs around it in the center of the space.

"The private dining room for the suites."

"You have a private dining room? I don't know why I'm surprised."

Jonathan chuckled. "It's just a small room with a table and some chairs."

"Yeah, but it's private. There isn't a lot of private space on this ship."

Before Jonathan could reply, the door opened behind him. Howard, Honey, and Ava walked into the room.

"Good morning," Howard said.

"Good morning," Jonathan replied.

"I'm starving," Honey said.

Jonathan tapped on the table. The menu appeared. After an awkward moment, everyone moved to take seats at the table. Howard sat on one end with Honey on one side and Ava on the other. Jonathan sat down opposite Howard. After a moment, I slid into the seat between Jonathan and Ava. Then I turned my attention to the menu. I found myself getting angry when I saw that half of the options were things that weren't available in the deck's dining room. Around me, everyone was making their selections. After a moment, I picked one of the options that I couldn't get in the dining room, even though it didn't really sound any better than any of the other options.

"Thank you for agreeing to talk to us," Jonathan said as the menu faded away after we'd all chosen.

Howard nodded. "I appreciate what you're trying to do. Putting Shawn Inmon in charge of the investigation is tantamount to telling the killer that he or she is free to go."

Jonathan chuckled. "Shawn will do his best. And he does have a bot working with him."

"Security bots are notoriously unreliable," Howard said. "They can handle simple tasks, but the intricacies of a murder investigation are beyond them. People are simply too complex for their programming."

"Are you sure it was murder?" Honey asked. "Maybe it was just an accident. Or maybe he had a heart attack or something."

"We're sure it was murder," Jonathan replied.

Howard nodded. "I suspected as much. Carl was smart. Too smart to wander into a bathroom and fall asleep. And even if he had, he wouldn't have stayed asleep while all of those alarms were going off. I figure he was either drugged and left there to die when the oxygen was shut off or he was already dead when the test started."

"How well did you know Carl?" Jonathan asked.

"We were friends. I know that isn't the public's perception of our relationship, but we were friends. Content creation is a tough business. It's made easier if you can find others who share your goals and ambitions and work together with them so that you can both succeed."

"You and Carl worked together?" I asked.

He shrugged. "Sometimes. He was already an established star when I first started in the business. I reached out to him for advice. He told me to make a particular short vid and the day I released it, he told everyone in the galaxy that it was dreadful. I was furious when I messaged him. He laughed and told me to take a look at my stats. That was the first content that I ever had go titanic on me. I fielded more than a dozen sponsorship offers that day and never looked back."

"So he launched your career," Jonathan said.

"I prefer to believe that he simply gave me a helping hand, that I would have been successful regardless, but my business definitely grew much more quickly thanks to his support. Even though that support seemed to be the opposite of support."

"And that support continued after that first time?" Jonathan asked.

"Not all the time, but occasionally. And it worked both ways. As I became more well known, I was able to return the favor on more than one occasion."

"And you always worked to create negative publicity for one another?" I asked.

"Not always. Sometimes one of us would grudgingly

admit that one of the other's newest content wasn't terrible," Howard said. "I went to one of his premieres once, back when he was making long-form content. And he came to my most recent premiere. Most of the content I create is released immediately, but very rarely I'll do an old-fashioned cinema release with a premiere and a red carpet. Carl came to the last one of those that I did. He walked out of the showing about halfway through, claiming the story had borrowed heavily from one of his earlier works. He threatened to sue, which was enough to take the release to the top of the charts for several weeks."

"But he wasn't serious?" I asked.

"Of course not," Howard said. "It was all a game, almost a chess match where we consulted one another before every move."

"Were you really going to be moving into immedieos?" Jonathan asked.

Howard sighed. "I hate rumors. I especially hate them when there is some truth behind them."

"Is that a yes?"

"Not exactly. I'm always exploring new concepts. One of the things that Honey and Ava have been doing on the *Lady Elizabeth* is playing with very short-form content."

"How short?" Jonathan asked.

"Something in the region of five minutes."

"So immedieos."

"But with fictional content. True fictional content, not the sort of semi-fictional sales-pitchy stuff that Carl was creating. I'm working on storytelling on a micro level. We've been trying to tell an entire story with five minutes of content. We've also been playing with five-minute clips that tie together to create a longer story, but that's been done before."

"Everything has been done before," Honey said. "Immedieos aren't anything new. They're just a different way of creating content and selling advertising."

Howard nodded. "What I want to do was never going to compete with what Carl was doing."

"Did you know Carl?" Jonathan asked Honey.

She shrugged. "I worked with him briefly years ago. I wrote maybe five things for him. I think he liked them all, but he was already moving away from long-form fictional content even then. When I finished my next project, I offered it to Howard first. He was happy to have it."

"And then I had her write me a dozen more things and I loved all of them," Howard said.

"I believe you worked with Zarina for a while," Jonathan said.

"She worked with Howard for a while. I was just the writer, who is pretty much insignificant once shooting has begun. That was still pretty early in my career, when I found it exciting to be on set while my work was being shot. That got old after a while, though."

"Do you enjoy being on set when your stories are being shot?" I asked Ava.

She shook her head. "It makes me uncomfortable, really," she said in a low voice.

"Howard, what do you think of Zarina?" Jonathan asked.

Before Howard could reply, the door opened, and a bot pushed a very full food trolley into the room. We all sat back as the bot began to put plates in front of us on the table.

"Do you require anything else in order to enjoy your meal?" the bot asked when the trolley was empty.

"We're good," Howard said.

The bot bobbed twice and then flew out the door, leaving the trolley behind. Everyone picked up their forks and began to eat.

"I thought she was a moderately talented actress with more ambition than talent," Howard said between bites. "She flirted with me when she first started working for me. When I made it clear that I wasn't interested, she moved on to Carl pretty quickly."

"Do you think she married him for his credits?" I asked.

Howard shook his head. "I think she married him for his influence. She wants to be a star. Once you have enough influence, the credits follow. I doubt Carl left her anything in his will. He told her he wasn't going to leave her anything when they got married. She didn't care. Marrying him, becoming a Seintruber, gave her a limitless well of credits and power that she can tap for the rest of her life."

"Did she kill him?" Jonathan asked.

"Maybe. I don't think she had anything to gain from his death, but she also had nothing to lose. She'd already secured his name for herself. Maybe she simply got tired of being married to him."

"She'll make a fortune sobbing about her tragic loss in immedieo after immedieo," Honey said. "But before she can do that, she's going to have to find someone to take care of the business side of her work. All she knows how to do is make five-minute clips. Carl did her editing and everything else from there on."

"She won't have any trouble finding a new producer," Howard said with a wave of his hand. "There are tons of eager beginners out there with the knowledge she needs. She'll be able to hire someone before we get to Galaxy Sector."

"What about Laresta?" Jonathan asked.

"She had something to gain from her father's death," Howard said. "She's going to inherit a fortune. She'll never have to work again if she doesn't want to."

"But she'll probably keep making content," Ava said. "She seems like the type to want to keep working, regardless."

"I wouldn't," Honey said. "If I inherited a fortune, I'd travel all over the galaxy in search of the best food credits can buy."

Ava shook her head. "I can't imagine not creating. Maybe I'd stop doing it for credits, but I'd still do it."

"Did any of you know Iris JaKay before she joined the ship?" Jonathan asked.

Howard made a face. "We'd met."

"And?"

He sighed. "I'm sure she'll tell you that I was quite horrible to her, but all I wanted to do was make a documentary about her planet and their unique language. Carl had just done exactly that, but as soon as I saw it, I realized that he'd allowed his affection for Iris to influence his content. It wasn't a documentary as much as a love letter to the galaxy about the planet and especially about Iris. I wanted to provide a more balanced view of the planet and its culture. Iris took steps to make sure that I was unable to do so."

"I'm sure that was difficult for you," Jonathan said.

"I was younger then, and quicker to anger. I got my revenge by making a docudrama on the planet. Except I couldn't shoot on the planet. And I couldn't persuade any Nadoians to be in it. I found a handful of actors who could speak Nado and we made the film on a neighboring planet that very closely resembled Nado, but it wasn't the same. And when the film came out, I discovered that the actors that I'd hired had been lying to me about their ability to use the Nado language. I was told that everything they say in the film is gibberish."

"It had a solid script," Honey said, winking at me.

Howard laughed. "It had a great script. And it went titanic in a big way because everyone in the galaxy was talking about it. And the very best part was that it was watched more on Nado than on any other planet. Everyone there wanted to try to understand what my actors were saying, or maybe they just wanted to laugh at the gibberish."

"How well do you know the various crew members who were there yesterday morning?" Jonathan asked.

Howard shrugged. "We met the captain back in Alpha Sector. He gave us a tour of the ship and arranged for us to use C Deck for some of the work we wanted to do."

"He's lovely," Honey said. "We've had dinner a few times. I've been trying to understand exactly why he wants to work in long-distance space travel. It seems a lonely existence for such a handsome man."

"He seems quite nice," Ava said.

"I've known Shawn for years, of course," Howard said. "More by reputation than anything else. I know his father rather better. Years ago, when I needed the credits, I shot some promotional stuff for InmonCorp. They still use clips from it in their advertising."

"What about Becca?" Jonathan asked.

"She's wonderful," Ava said.

Honey nodded. "Hiring her for this trip was the smartest thing InmonCorp could have done. She's exactly the person they need on a long-distance journey."

"I concur," Howard said.

"Troy?"

"Is an annoying man who is desperate to get back to Val

Segas where he was briefly moderately important," Howard said.

Honey shook her head. "He's not that bad. He's simply doing his job."

"I've no interest in buying any pictures, but I don't mind him taking them," Ava said.

"What about Craig Martelle?"

"He's scary," Honey said. "I always feel as if he's looking right through me when we talk."

"I think his sister scares me more," Ava said. "She's frighteningly smart and efficient."

"I admire them both very much," Howard said. "And I've tried to get both of them to agree to shooting something with me. They both refused. I'd very much like to work with you, too, Colonel."

Jonathan shook his head. "What about Shawn and Jerry?"

"If Shawn wanted someone dead, he'd get Jerry to eliminate the person. And Jerry would do so with clinical efficiency. The killer left too much to chance for it to have been Jerry's work," Howard said.

Jonathan nodded. "So, Howard, who do you think killed Carl?"

Howard frowned. "I wish I knew. I suppose I'm inclined to suggest Zarina simply because most people are killed by the person closest to them, but I really don't think she had motive." He sighed. "I suppose everyone else is pointing at me, but I didn't have a motive, either."

"Honey, same question," Jonathan said.

Honey shook her head. "I can't possibly answer that question."

"You've written murder mysteries," Howard said. "How would you wrap this one up?"

She frowned. "My murder mysteries always have an unexpected twist. I suppose if I were writing the story, one of the people in the room yesterday would have been Carl's long-lost sister or maybe a former wife or girlfriend. Or maybe a child that he never knew he'd fathered. Something like that, anyway."

"Assuming no unexpected twist, who do you think is the most likely suspect?" Jonathan asked.

"Maybe Jerry did it," she said after a moment. "Maybe he thought he was being clever by using the ship's fire-control system as a murder weapon. Maybe he actually was clever, because now he can claim that it was an accident, and it will be hard to prove otherwise."

Jonathan nodded. "Ava, what do you think?"

She tipped her head to one side and then shrugged. "I wish I knew. I hate to point fingers at anyone, but I suppose I agree with Howard. If I were you, I'd be looking at Zarina. Maybe she has someone else in her life and wanted out of her marriage without having to wait for a divorce to process."

"It would have been quite a process, if she had wanted to file now," Howard said. "Unless she and Carl both left the ship together, she would have had to wait until we got to Val Segas to file. And as I understand it, there aren't any other suites or cabins available on the ship now that so many people joined us on Caboluxous. She'd have been stuck in that suite with Carl for another twenty sectors."

"Thank you all for your time," Jonathan said. He put his empty plate on the trolley and looked at me. "Finished?" he asked.

I looked down at my empty plate. I barely remembered eating anything, but clearly I had. Nodding, I put my plate on the trolley and then followed Jonathan out of the room.

"That was interesting," he said when we got into the corridor.

"It was," I agreed. "Something is nagging at me, but I don't know what it is."

"Something someone said?"

"I guess so. I don't know."

"Maybe you'll figure it out if we talk about everyone."

"Maybe."

"Or we could..." He stopped when his comms buzzed. He read the screen and then looked at me.

"Or we could attend Carl's memorial service this afternoon and see what we can learn there," he said.

THIRTEEN

"There's a memorial service for Carl this afternoon?" I asked.

Jonathan nodded. "Just a small one for Carl's family and friends. Zarina isn't inviting the entire ship."

"Maybe she isn't inviting me."

"You're definitely invited. Check your comms."

I glanced at my wrist unit and discovered that it was dead. Sighing, I pulled out my comms. "Yeah, I'm invited," I said as I read the screen. "My wrist unit doesn't want to hold a charge for more than a few hours. It isn't usually a problem, because I'm usually just hanging out in my cabin so I can boost it any time."

"It's a pretty old unit."

"It's what I can afford."

"I probably have an old one somewhere that's newer than that one. I'll see if I can dig it out."

"Thank you, but I'm fine."

He frowned at me. "I don't need the old one. You might as well have it if I can find it."

"What are we going to do between now and the memorial service?"

"You probably have some studying to do. And we both need to have lunch."

I nodded. "So I'll see you in the private lounge — that I also didn't know the suite passengers had — around two?"

"If you're comfortable going on your own, sure. Otherwise, meet me at my suite a few minutes earlier and we can walk in together."

"I'll see you a few minutes before two, then," I said.

He nodded.

While I walked back to my cabin, I wondered what he had planned for the rest of his morning. Something that he clearly didn't want me to know about. But that was fine. We weren't even friends, not really. I opened my cabin door and grabbed Singer for a quick snuggle. Then I put a few minutes of effort into my study cube. My mind refused to focus, though. It kept replaying the various conversations that Jonathan and I had had with the suspects. I found myself pacing back and forth, annoying Singer, trying to figure out what was niggling at me. I gave up when my stomach started to grumble loudly.

The dining room felt oddly empty when I arrived. I was shown to a table for eight in the corner of the room. Only a handful of the other tables were occupied. I read through the menu and then ordered something almost at random. When I'd first arrived on the ship, I'd been excited by every meal. The food offered in the A Deck dining room was far superior to anything I'd eaten back on Cenclare, except on a handful of very special occasions in restaurants I really couldn't afford.

On the *Lady Elizabeth* meals were included, so I could enjoy all manner of fancy things, some of which I'd never tried before. My enthusiasm for the food started to wane by the time we'd reached Beta Sector. And now, four long sectors later, I felt as if I'd tried everything on the menu at least twice and that none of it was all that interesting.

"You're going to be broke and desperate again when you get to Val Segas," I muttered to myself. *"You really need to appreciate the food here more."*

I tried hard to enjoy every bite of my lunch when it arrived. Then I ordered a slice of chocolate cake for dessert. That, I enjoyed immensely. Feeling as if I'd been eating a bit too much cake lately, I took myself for a brisk walk around the deck. After three circuits, I decided that I'd worked hard enough for the day and went back to my cabin.

"What do you wear for a memorial service for a stranger?" I asked Singer.

She "mewed" at me. I sighed.

"I don't have that many clothes and none of them feel right. I suppose I could wear what I wore to Alan Royce's memorial service again. I wish I had limitless funds so that I could buy new clothes whenever I wanted them."

I pulled out the dark blue dress that I'd worn for the previous service. It was boring, but it would have to do.

"If I did have unlimited credits, I wouldn't buy a lot of clothes," I told Singer. "I don't usually pay much attention to what I wear. But it would be nice to be able to order a new dress for this memorial service. It's being held in the private lounge that I didn't know existed. Everyone else who will be there is staying in one of the suites. They all have loads of credits and they probably ordered new clothes just for today."

Singer yawned and then walked over and curled up on her pillow. I sighed and then finished getting ready to go to the service. I brushed my hair and added a few enhancers to my face before digging through my closet to find the shoes that most closely matched the dress. Then I dug out a handbag and dumped everything from my everyday bag into the blue bag that didn't exactly match anything else that I was wearing.

"It's going to have to do," I told Singer. "No one will be paying any attention to me, anyway."

I knocked on Jonathan's door a few minutes later.

"You look great," I said as I took in his dark grey suit. He was wearing a lighter grey shirt under it with an almost black tie.

"Thank you. So do you."

I shrugged. "I did my best."

We walked down the corridor, past the bar and the private dining room, to another unmarked door. Jonathan scanned his wrist unit and the door slid open. The room was an elegant lounge with large couches and chairs under graceful chandeliers that filled the room with diffused light. Zarina was sitting in a chair near the door. She stood up as we entered. Her dress was black, and she was wearing a black hat with a veil that covered her face.

"Thank you for coming," she said in a low voice. "It's very kind of you both to come to help me remember Carl."

"We're both very sorry for your loss," Jonathan said.

"I'm late," Laresta said as she walked in behind us. She looked around the room and then laughed. "But no one else is here yet, either."

"I'm here," Zarina said coldly.

"Yes, of course. And Colonel Brazee and Diana are here," Laresta said. "But they won't tell anyone that I was late."

"We're very sorry for your loss," Jonathan said.

She tilted her head to the side and then shrugged.

"Thank you. I'm still processing it, of course, but mostly I'm trying not to think about it. Except for the next hour or so, I have no choice but to think about it."

"We're going to be celebrating your father's life. It shouldn't be a sad time," Zarina said.

"But it's going to be sad," Laresta replied.

The door slid open again. Captain Ryder, in full dress uniform, strode into the room.

"Good afternoon," he said.

"Thank you for coming," Zarina said.

He nodded. "Very sorry for your loss."

The door opened again. Becca and Linda walked in together.

"I can't stay," Linda said. "I just wanted to come to pay my respects, as it were. But someone has to cover for Becca in the medical wing, just in case someone needs something. I just wanted to tell you both how sorry I am for your loss."

She nodded at Zarina and then Laresta.

"Thank you," Zarina said.

"Yeah, thanks," Laresta said.

"Message me if you need me," Becca told Linda.

"I will," Linda replied. She gave me a quick smile before she left the room.

"How did you sleep last night?" Becca asked Zarina.

"Fitfully. I kept waking up, expecting to see Carl next to me. And then reality would come flooding back and I'd start crying again."

"I can give you something to help you sleep for a few nights," Becca offered.

Zarina shook her head. "I think I need to deal with reality sooner rather than later."

"How are you?" Becca asked Laresta.

"I got too drunk to care about anything yesterday and

then slept like a rock. Today, I'm pretending that this is all just a bad dream. The longer I can keep reality at a distance, the better," she replied.

"Everyone deals with tragedy differently. You know where to find me if you want some extra support."

The door opened again. Craig and Tammy walked into the room. Jonathan and I moved out of the way as they both spoke briefly to Zarina and Laresta. As they moved toward the couches, the door opened again. Howard, Honey, and Ava were all dressed in black from head to toe.

"We're very sorry for your loss," Howard said to Zarina. The two women both nodded. Then he looked at Laresta. "And we're very sorry for your loss," he said.

She nodded. "Thank you."

For a moment, no one spoke. Then the door opened, and Iris walked in.

"I'm so very sorry," she said. Her arms and hands moved gracefully as she said a few words to Zarina and then to Laresta. Jonathan and I moved farther from the door as Howard, Honey, and Ava walked farther into the room.

"Is everyone here?" Zarina asked as Iris headed for one of the couches.

As I looked around, the door opened again. Shawn and Jerry joined us.

"I hope we're not late," Shawn said. "I lost track of time. I do that a lot."

"Thank you for coming," Zarina said.

"I didn't think I had a choice," Shawn replied, looking confused. He glanced at Jerry, who sighed deeply.

"I don't want this to be anything too formal," Zarina said, taking a step away from the door. "I just want it to be a celebration of Carl's life. A small and intimate celebration for today. In a few days, after I've had time to process some of what I'm feeling, we'll have another service so that everyone on the *Lady Elizabeth* will have a chance to celebrate Carl's life with me. But for today, I wanted to keep it small. This is about all that I can deal with at the moment."

The door opened. Troy walked in and looked around. "Hi," he said with an awkward wave.

Zarina nodded at him. "We were just about to start," she said. "I want to share a few memories of Carl with you all."

Those of us who were still standing moved over to take seats on the couches. Zarina stood between them and then very slowly rotated in place. I could see tears sliding down her cheeks as she inhaled slowly.

"I met Carl at a party," she began.

Twenty minutes later, I was struggling to stay awake. Zarina's voice seemed to drone on and on as she told us far more about her relationship with Carl than I wanted to know. When she paused between stories, Jonathan spoke in my ear.

"Poke me every time she says 'Carl.' Maybe that will keep us both awake."

I hid my laugh in a cough as Zarina began to speak again. After another ten minutes, she finally stopped.

"I could keep talking all afternoon and into the evening. But some of my memories of Carl might be best kept to myself. And I'll share more at the larger service as well. I think it's probably time to hear from someone else. Laresta?"

Laresta got to her feet. She cleared her throat and then shrugged. "I don't know what to say. My father was a complicated man. I think he did his best to be a good father to me, but he was also very busy. There were many months during my childhood when I never saw him, not even over comms. But he loved and was devoted to his work. And I respect that. I'm much the same. I love what I do. I'm not sure I can imagine doing it without his support, though."

"I'll do everything I can to help," Howard said.

She beamed at him. "That's very kind of you."

"The offer extends to you, too, Zarina," Howard said. "Carl was my friend. I want to do what I can to support his widow and his daughter."

"Thank you," Zarina said. "I'm not ready to start thinking about work yet, but I will be soon."

Howard nodded. Everyone turned their attention back to Laresta.

"I don't know what else to say. I should have stories for you from my childhood, but you don't need to hear about my life with my nannies."

"But you are grateful to your father for supporting your career," Zarina said.

"Oh, yes, of course. And over the past few years my father and I were able to develop a relationship that was based on working together. I'm going to miss him very much."

Laresta sat down and then wiped her eyes with a tissue.

"Howard, would you like to say a few words?" Zarina asked.

Howard nodded. He stood up and looked around the room. "Carl and I were friends who did everything we could to support one another. That support most often took the guise of generating negative publicity for one another, which convinced much of the galaxy that we were enemies. Nothing could have been further from the truth, though."

He told everyone the story he'd told Jonathan and me about the early days of his career. Then he told a few more stories about times when Carl had been critical of his work.

"Every time Carl said something negative about what I was doing, my views would skyrocket. And the same was true for him when I was critical of what he was doing. And we had frequent conversations in the bar here, on the *Lady Elizabeth,* about how we could continue to drive viewers to one another. We were by no means finished supporting each other's careers. I'm sad and angry that we will not be able to work together in the future."

Zarina began to rotate again. "Does anyone else want to say anything?" she asked.

Iris got to her feet. "Carl was a dear friend," she said, her hand gestures seeming to radiate sadness. "We worked together on a project that was important to his business but was also important to me and to my planet. The best thing that came out of that documentary, though, was my friendship with Carl. Over the decades since we worked together, we remained in contact, spoke frequently, and saw each other whenever we could manage it. I'm going to miss him terribly."

She sat down and buried her head in her hands. Captain Ryder, who was sitting next to her, handed her a tissue.

"Anyone else?" Zarina asked.

Honey stood up. "I didn't work with Carl for long, but I very much enjoyed doing the handful of projects with him that I did. He was an amazing content producer and had he opted to continue with long-form content, I'd like to think that we would have continued to work together for many more years. I'm grateful that I did have a chance to work with him, however briefly, and I'm very sorry for your loss," she told Zarina.

"Thank you," Zarina said. She looked around again. "Does anyone else want to say anything?" she asked.

Tammy got up. She looked around the room and then sighed deeply. "Carl was a wonderful person. I cared about him, and I'm very sorry that he's gone." She shared a memory of having dinner with Carl at a restaurant in Val Segas. During their meal, just about everyone who was anyone in the galaxy took a moment to stop at their table to have a word with Carl.

"He was someone special. He will be missed," she finally concluded.

This time, when Zarina asked if anyone else wanted to speak, no one moved. She did another slow rotation before taking a deep breath.

"I don't want to prolong this unnecessarily, but I also don't want this to end," she said. "Everything that happens, every sunrise, every sunset, every meal, every gathering like this one, is another thing that moves me farther and farther away from Carl. I feel as if I need to stay right here, in this space, for as long as possible. You were all with me when Carl's body was found. I feel closer to him with you around me than I do when I'm alone in our suite, even though we shared that suite. I'm sorry. I just don't want to ever be alone again."

As she broke down in tears, Becca got up and walked to her.

"There's cake," Laresta said after an awkward moment when the sound of Zarina's sobbing seemed to fill the room.

Zarina looked up from Becca's arms. "Yes, there's cake. Vanilla cake with sprinkles. It was Carl's favorite. Please, have some."

After a moment, everyone started to get up and shuffle toward the table in the corner. Dozens of slices of cake were laid out on small plates across the surface of the table. A hot-drinks machine hummed in the corner.

Troy was the first to reach the table. He picked up a piece of cake and then pushed more than a dozen buttons on the drink machine. Eventually, it began to click and whir before a cup dropped down and slowly filled with some frothy brown liquid. The rest of us followed, getting cake slices and then programming our own drinks.

Becca walked back with her arm around Zarina. She took one look at all of us, standing around awkwardly trying to juggle plates full of cake and hot drinks, and then walked to the wall and tapped in a command. A moment later a pair of tables slowly began to lift out of the floor. Everyone rushed toward them, eager to put their plates and mugs down. I found myself standing between Honey and Ava when everyone had finally found a space.

"Do you want to switch places?" I asked Ava.

She made a face and then tipped her head to the side before shrugging. "I'm fine here. Honey and I are good friends, but we both can talk to other people."

I nodded. "I didn't mean to suggest otherwise," I said.

"This is all very sad," Honey said. "I feel so sorry for Zarina."

"She'll be fine," Ava said. "She's probably going to be a very rich widow, but regardless, she'll be able to make a fortune from the Seintruber name, anyway."

"I feel sorry for Laresta," I said. "Maybe she'll reach out to her mother now that her father is gone."

"She might not even know where to find her," Ava said.

"It's a small galaxy," Honey said. "No one is all that hard to find."

Ava shrugged.

"I hope you are all enjoying your cake," Zarina said. "As I mentioned, it was Carl's favorite. I'm sure he'd be thrilled to know that you're enjoying his favorite thing."

"You should have given them all scotch," Laresta said. "He liked scotch a lot more than he liked cake."

Zarina frowned at the other woman. "Let's not argue. Not now."

"Who's arguing? You can't argue with facts," Laresta shot back.

"Thank you for including me in the service," Iris said, stepping between the two women. "I don't believe that I'll ever stop missing Carl, but I'm comforted by the idea that lived his life surrounded by people who loved him."

Zarina nodded. "I loved him very much."

"Ha," Laresta said.

"We should talk," Howard said to Laresta. "I want you to teach me about immedieos. Let's go to the bar and talk there."

Laresta hesitated and then nodded. "Sure, let's do that," she said.

We all watched as she and Howard walked out of the room together.

"We should probably go, too," Honey said to Ava as the door shut behind them. "If Howard does actually learn anything, he's going to want us to know it too."

Ava sighed. "Or we could just have one afternoon off from Howard and work."

Honey raised an eyebrow. "Why don't you go and rest. I'll go and have a drink with Howard and Laresta."

"I'm sorry. I have a headache again. I haven't been sleeping well for the last few sectors. Are you sure you don't mind going alone?"

"I won't be alone. I'll be with Howard and Laresta."

The two women walked out of the room together. Captain Ryder left right behind them. Craig and Tammy followed him a moment later. Iris finished her cake and left without saying another word. Jonathan touched my shoulder a moment later.

"Ready to go?" he asked me.

I nodded. "More than."

Becca was still talking to Zarina as we headed for the door. Troy was steadily working his way through a second slice of cake. Shawn and Jerry were having a conversation together on the opposite side of the room. I glanced at them as Jonathan and I walked back into the corridor.

"Now what?" I asked.

"Now I want to go through the photos that Troy took yesterday. Maybe they picked up something that we missed."

FOURTEEN

Jonathan and I walked together to his cabin. Inside, I sat down on the couch and then sighed.

"Have you found Natalie, then?" I asked.

He laughed. "No, I haven't, actually. Let's do that now, shall we?"

I nodded. He walked over to his computer and scrolled through a few screens. After a minute, I walked over to join him.

"I don't know anyone who lives on Florzonia, but that doesn't mean I don't have any contacts there," he said.

A moment later, a man appeared on the screen. He smiled broadly.

"Colonel Brazee, this is an honor," he said.

"Detective Markham, good afternoon."

"What can the Florzonia Safety and Security Force do for you, Colonel?"

"I'm trying to locate Natalie Seintruber. I don't actually need to speak to her. I simply need to know that she's on-planet."

The detective typed something into the computer next

to him on his desk. "I'm not finding anyone with that name in our systems."

"She might have gone back to using her previous name. She was Natalie Vanderdorf before she got married."

The man nodded. "Ah, yes. I've found her. And Seintruber is listed as one of her aliases. She should have come up when I searched under that name. I'm going to have to talk to someone to find out why it didn't."

"As I said, I just need to know if she's on-planet."

"She lives in Floze, which is our capital city and where I'm stationed, so it shouldn't take me long to verify that she's here. How classified is your inquiry?"

"I don't care if she knows that someone was asking questions about her whereabouts. Her former husband was just murdered. She should understand that she could be a person of interest in the investigation."

"Where was her husband when he died?"

"On the *Lady Elizabeth* en route to Val Segas."

The man made a face. "I've been hearing a lot about the *Lady Elizabeth* since she blasted off from Cenclare. Quite a lot of your passengers seem to be getting murdered."

"Don't believe everything you hear," Jonathan told him.

"I think I'll take this one myself. It shouldn't take long. I'll tag you when I have something to report."

"Thanks."

"No problem. Happy to help, Sir."

Jonathan looked at me. "Happy now?"

"It's just a loose end," I said. "She's probably wandering around Florzonia, blissfully unaware that I'm somewhat obsessed with her whereabouts."

"Let's take a look at the pictures that Troy took on the day of the murder."

He clicked through several screens and then opened a

folder. The screen filled with a badly framed picture of a man about to put a piece of bacon into his mouth. Jonathan moved to the next picture. It was the same man, frowning at the camera. In the third picture, he was shaking his fist and starting to stand up. The fourth picture was of a smiling woman.

I laughed. "Troy moved to the other side of the dining room after the third picture," I said.

Jonathan nodded. "It looks as if he started near the door and then moved to the very back of the room." He scrolled through what felt like hundreds more photographs of people having breakfast. Following those were a few pictures that had been taken in the A Deck lounge. I smiled as I spotted a familiar face.

Carolyn Henry was sitting comfortably on one of the couches as it floated past the camera. As usual, she was knitting. The picture also captured Carolyn's cat peeking its head out of one of the bags on the couch next to the woman.

"Here we are," Jonathan said. "Troy took a lot of pictures in the C Deck hallway on his way to the safety test."

"I wonder why."

"Maybe he was just excited to be on C Deck."

"Maybe."

"Or maybe they're going to be part of his exposé."

Jonathan stopped scrolling when we reached the first picture that had been taken inside Cabin C166. We both stared at the picture that showed everyone assembled in the cabin. A loud buzzing noise made me jump.

"Ah, that's Detective Markham," Jonathan said.

The man's face filled the screen again.

"No one is at home at Ms. Vanderdorf's residence, but I spoke to her neighbor. According to the woman who lives next door, Ms. Vanderdorf travels a great deal, but never very far. When questioned, she stated for the record that she saw Ms. Vanderdorf going into her house yesterday or maybe the day before."

Jonathan frowned. "I want to talk to her," he said.

The detective looked surprised. "We've never had reason to question the woman's honesty. She's a native Florzonian and a biomedical researcher at our largest hospital."

"I want to talk to her," Jonathan said again.

The man nodded. "Give me a minute to set things up on this end."

The screen went dark. Jonathan glanced at me.

"It's probably nothing," he said.

"But it could be something."

"It could be."

The buzzing noise made me jump a second time. Detective Markham reappeared.

"Here's Aurora Night," he said before a woman took his place on the screen. She was a pretty blonde who looked nervous.

"Good afternoon," Jonathan said.

"It's morning here," she replied. "And I'm going to be late for work if this takes too long."

"I only have a few questions," Jonathan said. "You told Detective Markham that Natalie travels a lot. How often and for how long does she typically travel?"

The woman shook her head. "We're neighbors, not friends. We exchange polite greetings if we happen to cross paths, but we don't really talk. I know she travels because I see her going in and out with suitcases from time to time. I asked her about her travels once and she said she likes to spend time on the other side of the planet. It's cooler and wetter there. Many people who live in Floze like to spend time on that side of the planet."

"Just one more question, then. Please think very carefully before you answer. You must know that lying to an officer investigating a murder is a criminal offense."

The woman paled visibly. "Murder?"

"When did you last see Natalie?" Jonathan asked.

"I'm not sure. I don't keep track of her comings and goings."

"You told Detective Markham that you saw her yesterday or the day before."

"Approximately."

"How approximately?"

She sighed. "I don't know. As I said, I don't keep track of her. I've been really busy with work, and I've been working really odd hours, which means we haven't crossed paths in quite a while. I'm not sure how long it's been, though."

"Did she ever ask you to lie on her behalf if you were questioned by Safety and Security?"

The woman squirmed in her seat. "I really need to get to work."

"I'd like you to look at a picture and tell me if you recognize anyone," Jonathan said. He tapped the screen and then pulled up the photo of everyone in cabin C166.

"No," the woman said, clearly relieved. "I mean, I do recognize Shawn Inmon, because he's Shawn Inmon. And I recognize Howard Howard, because everyone knows Howard Howard. A few of the others look vaguely familiar. Some of them might be content creators, but I don't watch a lot of screen. My job keeps me pretty busy."

"You're certain?"

She shrugged. "It isn't difficult to change your appearance. If you're asking if anyone in the picture could be

Natalie, then sure. Any of the women and a few of the men look enough like her to be possibilities. It wouldn't take more than a few inexpensive changes to make Natalie unrecognizable to me, especially considering how infrequently we see one another."

"Are there any other neighbors who are better friends with Natalie?"

She shook her head. "We're on a dead-end street. Natalie's is the last house. I'm her only neighbor on this side of the street and there's a mall on the opposite side of the street."

"Thank you for your time." Jonathan said.

"I can go?"

"For now."

A moment later Detective Markham returned. "I have a copy of Ms. Vanderdorf's most recent identity photo, if you think that would help," he said.

"Let's see it."

I stared at the screen. The woman looked very ordinary, with long grey hair and thick glasses. I sighed and shook my head.

"Thank you. I might be in touch with more questions later," Jonathan said.

"You know where to find me. I was happy to help," the man replied.

As the screen went black, I looked at Jonathan.

"It could be Ava or Honey," I said.

He nodded. "Let's go through the photos and see what we can find."

"If one of them is actually Natalie, then surely Laresta knows who she really is."

"Maybe. There are a lot of possibilities."

Jonathan began to scroll through the pictures again. I

stared at them while my mind raced. We were nearly to the end when I gasped.

"That's it," I said.

"What?"

"Go back."

Jonathan clicked back to the previous photo. I stared at Ava.

"Leave that one on the screen and go back to the pictures Troy took of Laresta," I said.

Jonathan did as I asked. I watched for what I thought I'd seen.

"There. That one."

Jonathan put the two pictures side by side.

"They both do the same thing," I said. "They both tilt their heads and then shrug. It's almost like they're related. That's what has been nagging at me since we first spoke to them both."

Jonathan studied the pictures. "It is the exact same gesture, but it proves nothing."

"Ava is Natalie," I said.

"You sound certain."

"I am certain."

He sighed. "Let's go and talk to Ava."

"If we can get her away from Howard and Honey."

"I can do that."

Jonathan sent a message. A short while later, he had a reply.

"Let's go."

"Where?"

"Ava wants to speak to us in her suite."

The suite was only a few doors away. Ava opened the door to Jonathan's knock.

"You have more questions for me?" she asked, looking confused.

Jonathan nodded. "I want to talk to you about your daughter."

Ava shook her head. "I don't have any children."

"Can we come in?" Jonathan asked.

"Oh, of course. I'm sorry. I was so surprised by your request that I forgot my manners."

She stepped backward to let us into the suite. The living room felt larger than Jonathan's, with one huge horseshoe-shaped couch.

"Have a seat," she said, gesturing toward the couch.

Jonathan and I walked over and sat down.

"It was Diana who spotted it," Jonathan said.

"Spotted what?"

"The way you tilt your head and then shrug. Your daughter does the exact same thing."

"I just told you. I don't have any children."

"I'm investigating a murder. I can legally require both you and Laresta to take DNA tests," Jonathan said.

Ava pressed her lips together for a moment and then sighed. "I'm not sure why I'm worried. Carl is gone. He can't keep us apart any longer."

"He kept you apart?" I asked.

She gave me a sad smile. "I'm sure you've been told otherwise. Carl was a master of controlling his own publicity. He made sure that the entire galaxy thought that I'd abandoned my baby girl."

"What really happened?" Jonathan asked.

She started to tilt her head and then stopped herself before shrugging. "I was young and stupid. No, that isn't fair. I was young and naïve. I thought I was marrying a man who loved me and wanted to spend forever with me. I was wrong."

"I'm sorry," I said as I watched tears fill her eyes.

"We both wanted children. Carl originally wanted a dozen. I told him that I didn't want to commit to that many, not until after we'd had our first. I know that having children sometimes changes people. It changed Carl."

As tears began to slide down her cheeks, I looked around the room for a box of tissues. I spotted one behind Jonathan and pointed to it. He didn't seem to understand me, though. Sighing, I got to my feet and grabbed the box before holding it out to Ava. She wiped her eyes.

"I consented to only a single embryo. I couldn't bear the thought of creating all of that potential life and then not allowing every embryo to fulfill its potential. And, if I'm honest, I was already having doubts about my marriage. Carl was less and less interested in me every day. He took a trip for many months with his closest friend, Iris. I wasn't supposed to be jealous of their relationship, even though they spent considerably more time together than Carl and I did."

"Do you think they had an affair?"

She shrugged. "I know they became emotionally connected. In my mind that's worse than if they'd had a physical affair. They might have done both. I don't know."

"What happened, then?"

"We created our embryo. It tested healthy, so we had it incubated. And then Carl became obsessed. He spent hours and hours at the laboratory, visiting the incubation chamber. He used to go and talk to the baby and rub the chamber. I know that both of those things are good for the developing baby, but the lab had a team of specialists who were tasked with doing both of those jobs throughout the day. Our technician told me privately that mostly Carl was just getting in the way."

I frowned. "They didn't want the parents to visit?"

"They were happy for us to visit, but each set of parents was assigned certain visiting hours on certain days. The clinic asked that we stick to those in order to limit the number of visitors at any given time. Carl simply went whenever he wanted to see the baby. And he wanted to see the baby all the time."

"How did you feel about the baby?" I asked.

She smiled. "Ambivalent. And more than a little scared. It was one thing when the baby was in her incubator, growing slowly. The idea of bringing her home and being responsible for another living being was quite terrifying. Oh, I knew that we'd have plenty of help, but the idea of being a mother was hard for me to process. My own mother hated her children and never missed an opportunity to remind us of that fact. As the baby got bigger, I started to worry that I'd be the same with my daughter."

She stopped and wiped her eyes again.

"It's okay," I said.

"It's ancient history, anyway. Carl and I were drifting apart. He didn't think I was spending enough time with the baby. I thought he was spending too much time with her. It was obvious that our marriage wasn't going to survive for much longer. And then the clinic gave us our date."

"Laresta's birth date?" Jonathan asked.

She nodded. "Carl set up the nursery and hired a team of people to attend to her every need. We were together when the incubator was opened. They handed her straight to Carl. I looked at her and felt a huge rush of love and affection and a dozen other emotions that I couldn't even understand. I wanted to hold her so badly, but Carl wouldn't let her go. Eventually, the doctors insisted on taking her away for some initial evaluations. By the time I got to hold her, she'd been cleaned up and put into the little outfit that Carl had brought for her."

"I hope it was a special moment," I said.

"It was an incredibly special moment. I held her close and kissed her tiny nose. It didn't seem possible that she was really mine. I had considered carrying her myself, but Carl wanted to use the clinic. Of course that's much safer for both mother and baby, but I do feel as if I missed out on something by not carrying her. Regardless, I loved her dearly."

"What went wrong?"

"Things had already gone badly wrong. I just didn't know how badly until the baby came home. As I said, Carl had hired an entire team of people to take care of Laresta. Every time I tried to visit, I was told that she was too tired or hungry or grumpy or something. I got sent away time and time again, told to come back later. Carl, of course, used to visit her whenever he wanted. No one dared tell him that he couldn't see her. When I complained to Carl, he just laughed and told me that his team would do a better job of raising Laresta than I would, anyway. And I was so miserable and unhappy that I found myself agreeing with him."

"So you left," Jonathan said.

"It wasn't that easy. I told Carl that I wasn't happy. He told me that he wasn't going to do a single thing to improve my life. When I asked for the divorce, he gave me two choices. I could fight him in the courts for Laresta. If I chose to fight, he'd give me custody and then cut me off without a single credit to my name. Laresta and I would have been homeless and alone in the galaxy."

"Surely he would have had to pay something for support," I said.

"We'd signed an agreement before we got married. I agreed that I would get nothing if we divorced, regardless of the circumstances," she replied. "I did it to prove to him that I wasn't after his credits. I never realized, at the time, that I was also signing away my rights to my daughter."

"What was your other option?"

"I could give him full custody of the baby. In return, he would give me enough credits to set up a new life somewhere else. And Laresta would be given the best possible life that he could give her."

"So you chose what was best for her," I said.

"I chose what I thought was best for her. It broke my heart. I moved to Florzonia and didn't leave my house for three years. Eventually, I started pouring my sorrow into stories. Those stories caught Howard's eye. My plan, when I started working for him, was to make enough credits to be able to give Carl my settlement back and demand a relationship with my daughter."

"What happened?"

"Carl happened," she said bitterly.

FIFTEEN

"What does that mean?" I asked.

"Carl found out what I was doing, and he told Howard that he'd stop supporting him if he kept working with me. Howard was very apologetic, but he didn't have much choice but to end his relationship with me."

"So you changed your identity," Jonathan said.

She shook her head. "I simply adopted a pen name. There's a long literary tradition of authors using names other than their own. I started writing under three different names. Howard was kind enough to pretend not to realize. We worked together to keep Carl from finding out."

"Coming on the *Lady Elizabeth* was a huge risk," I said.

"And I'm beyond caring now. I've built up my own small fortune in credits. And Laresta is an adult. She gets to make her own decisions about who gets to be a part of her life. The last several years have been increasingly frustrating as I've watched Laresta grow up on screen. I've traveled from one side of the galaxy to the other, trying to cross paths with her. Carl kept very strict control over her movements and access to her. When I found out that he was going to be taking the *Lady Elizabeth* to Val Segas, I could barely contain myself."

"So you booked yourself a suite?" I asked.

"I couldn't risk that. Ava Ross is just a pen name. All of my accounts are in my real name. What I did was go to Howard and beg him to arrange everything."

"And he did."

"He was already considering using the *Lady Elizabeth* to get back to Val Segas. He's shooting a new docudrama about gambling there after we arrive. The man backing that project paid for our tickets on the *Lady Elizabeth*."

"For all three of you?" Jonathan asked.

She nodded. "Honey and I are writing the script for the docudrama. It's going to be heavy on drama."

"Surely you were taking a huge risk, traveling on the same ship with your former husband," I said.

She laughed. "I had work done. I had so much done that I no longer recognize myself. I only had temporary adjustments made. Some will fade over time. Others can be easily reversed. I haven't been maintaining them, and I've already noticed a difference. Now that Carl is gone, I no longer have to worry about them at all. I might see if Becca can reverse some of them for me soon."

"So Carl didn't recognize you. When did you introduce yourself to Laresta?" Jonathan asked.

"We first met in Alpha Sector. She was so beautiful and she's amazingly talented, too. I knew that, of course, because I've seen every second of screen that she's ever done, but meeting her in person was different. Of course, I had to act as if I barely knew who she was. Inside, though, I was screaming."

"When did you tell Laresta who you were?" Jonathan asked.

"It took time. First, I had to get to know her a bit. I started out just saying hi to her when we crossed paths somewhere on the ship. Then I started making small talk with her. Eventually, I had a few short conversations with her. It wasn't until Delta Sector that I mentioned her mother. She immediately told me all of the lies that her father had filled her head with since the day she was born. I just reminded her that there are two sides to every story." She stopped talking, a faraway look in her eyes.

"What did she say to that?" I asked.

"She just laughed and said she didn't need to hear her mother's side of the story, that her mother was dead to her."

"That must have hurt," I said.

"It hurt a great deal, but it also let me know what I was up against. I spent the rest of that sector and part of the next getting to know her better. It was never easy to talk to her, because her father kept a very close eye on her, but over time he seemed to stop seeing me as a threat. By the time we reached Caboluxous, he was willing to let Laresta visit the planet with me and Honey instead of with him and Zarina."

"I'm sure Zarina didn't mind," I said.

Ava smiled. "She was my biggest ally, even though she didn't know she was helping me. She saw how much Carl doted on Laresta and decided that giving Carl another baby would get her more of his time and attention. She was badly wrong, of course, but now she'll never know."

"When did you finally tell her who you were?" I asked.

"I hinted at it for ages, but she never realized. It wasn't until the last day in Energy Sector that I was finally able to say something. When we left Caboluxous, I dropped something of mine in her bag. When she spotted it, she messaged me. I invited her to my cabin so that she could return it. When she got here, I was ready for her."

"Ready?" Jonathan echoed.

She nodded and then got up and walked to the screen on the wall. She turned it on and then tapped through a few menus before selecting something. The screen filled with a baby picture, presumably of Laresta. Jonathan and I watched as pictures came and went. The narration told the story that Ava had just shared with us.

"She didn't want to believe me, of course. She accused me of just being after her credits. I assured her that I have plenty of credits of my own. She watched what I'd prepared twice and then she left. She was upset and angry, but I still don't know if she believed me."

"You haven't spoken to her since?"

"We haven't had a chance to talk. I tried reaching out to her after her father's death, but she hasn't responded."

"She must have been really upset," I said. "You called into question everything she's ever believed about her life."

Ava nodded. "She said she wanted to confront her father and get the real story from him. Sadly, I don't think she ever got the chance."

Jonathan shook his head. "She had more than enough time to talk to him before his death. She wouldn't have waited. I suspect she confronted him later that same day."

"If she had, Carl would have been banging on my door, furious with me."

"Maybe she did wait," I said. "Maybe she waited until she had things arranged the way she wanted before she said anything."

Jonathan nodded. "There were quite a few things that had to be put into place."

Ava frowned. "What are you talking about?"

"Thank you for your time," Jonathan said, getting to his

feet. "Please don't say anything to anyone about this conversation."

"I won't. I'm not ready to be Natalie Vanderdorf again just yet."

I got up and followed Jonathan to the door. As he reached for the button to open it, Ava spoke again.

"What do you think Laresta arranged?" she asked.

Jonathan turned around and gave her a sympathetic smile. "We're still investigating," he said.

I watched the color drain from Ava's cheeks. "That isn't – you can't be suggesting – she was upset, but – it's not possible. She loved her father."

"Maybe."

Ava rushed over and grabbed Jonathan's arm. "I did it," she said.

He shook his head.

"I did. I set everything up. Honey and I have had the run of all of C Deck for ages. We've been in and out of every cabin at least twice. When we were invited to the fire system safety test, I went down and inspected the cabin where the test was going to be held. I rigged the bathroom door so that it could only be opened from the outside. Then I invited Carl to meet me at the cabin before the test was scheduled to start. We talked for a short while and then I asked him to get me some tissues from the bathroom. As soon as he went inside, I shut the door, locking him in. Then I just had to wait for the test to start. As soon as they shut off the oxygen supply to the cabin, I knew I'd killed Carl."

Jonathan frowned. "There are a lot of elements in your story that don't match the evidence."

"Give me another chance," Ava pleaded.

"We need to go and talk to Laresta now," Jonathan said.

"But I'm putting you under arrest before we do that, just in case."

"Just in case?"

He pulled out his comms. When the knock on the door came, Jonathan opened it to a team of security bots.

"Take her to a holding area until further notice. Total ban on external communication."

Ava followed the bots into the corridor. "Please believe me. I killed Carl. Laresta didn't do anything. Please," she said through tears.

"We'll talk later," Jonathan said.

We stood and watched as the bots led her away. Jonathan sighed.

"She's going to be heartbroken when she finds out that Laresta did it," I said.

"I really thought Ava did it," Jonathan said. "I thought when I told her that I was going to talk to Laresta that she'd confess, but I also thought her confession would be true."

"Maybe she's smart enough to get the details wrong to further complicate things."

"Maybe. Let's see what Laresta has to say."

They walked the short distance to the woman's cabin. Jonathan knocked. Laresta opened the door a moment later.

"Colonel Brazee? This is a surprise. I hope you've come to suggest a trip to the bar. I haven't had a drink in hours."

"I have a few questions for you," Jonathan said. "Can we come in?"

Some emotion, maybe fear, flashed over her face before she smiled and took a step backward. "Of course," she said.

Her living room looked a lot like Ava's, with the large semicircle of a couch in the center.

"Please, sit," she said. "This is all very exciting. When

you're done asking me questions, I'd love to ask you a few. I could use a few incredible soundblips from you."

"I'm not interested," Jonathan said. "I just had an interesting conversation with your mother."

I watched Laresta's face. She seemed to be calculating how best to respond.

"My mother? She's on the ship? I wasn't aware," she said eventually. "I have no interest in hearing what she had to say."

"She's confessed to killing your father."

Laresta looked shocked and then pleased. "She has? That's actually quite interesting. They got divorced a long time ago. Why would she kill him now?"

"She didn't."

"I'm confused."

"She confessed because she wanted to protect someone she loves."

Laresta frowned. "According to my father, my mother never loved anyone other than herself."

"But you know that isn't true. She told you so herself."

Again, I could see the woman weighing up her possible responses.

"You've been talking to Ava," she said eventually. "We had a conversation or two. She tried to convince me that she was my mother. I was going to ask my father about it, but sadly I never got the opportunity."

"Why not just take DNA tests?" Jonathan asked. "Becca could have processed them in minutes."

Laresta shook her head. "I wasn't ready for proof, not yet. My father told me very little about my mother over the years, but I knew enough to question everything that Ava said to me, at least. I was fascinated by what she said, but I didn't really believe her."

"So you never talked to your father about Ava?"

"I never got the chance."

"He would have been angry to know that you'd spoken to her."

She shrugged. "Probably. He did his best to keep us apart. He did it for my good, though. My mother never really loved me."

"Ava has evidence to the contrary," Jonathan said. "She's kept pictures of you from the day you emerged. And she's followed your career as much as she could. She's so devoted to you that she confessed to killing your father out of fear that you killed him."

Laresta's smile was sly. "I can't believe that she killed him, but maybe I shouldn't be surprised. She was so angry with him for keeping us apart for so many years."

"So you did believe her."

"I'm not saying that. I believe that she thought that she was my mother. People sometimes have false memories. Or maybe she met my mother, heard her story, and decided to pretend to be her in order to try to get some credits from me or my father." She tipped her head to the side and shrugged. "You can understand why I wasn't sure what to think. There are so many possibilities."

Jonathan nodded. "I'm surprised you didn't talk to your father immediately."

"I needed to do some research, to find out as much as I could about Ava. But that was a dead end. It's just her pen name, not her real name."

"And you had to research the ship's systems," Jonathan said.

She blinked several times. "Why would I need to do that?"

"You were going to do some immedieos about the fire-control system test, weren't you?"

"Oh, yes, of course," she said, looking relieved.

Jonathan sat back in his seat. "It should be fairly easy to trace the drugs that you used back to you."

"No way. I stole those from – I mean, I don't know what you're talking about."

He nodded. "You confronted your father in cabin C166 before the test was due to start, didn't you? What did he say? Did he try to deny that he'd done everything in his power to keep you and your mother apart?"

Laresta slowly shook her head, clearly trying to think. Finally, she sighed. "I did talk to him that morning about my mother. I needed to hear his side of the story, but, of course, I'd been hearing his side of the story for my entire life. When I told him that I'd talked to my mother, he got angry. He demanded to know who she was so that he could confront her. I was afraid for Ava's life."

"That's a very solid stance," Jonathan said. "You should go with that."

"Thanks," Laresta said, smiling smugly.

"So what happened next?" Jonathan asked.

"He was angry, shouting, screaming about how I didn't understand. I wanted him to calm down, so I gave him something to drink. I just wanted him to go to sleep for an hour or so, until the test was over. I was going to warn Ava after the test was over so that she could hide from my father."

"So you drugged your father."

"Just a little bit. Just to make him sleep through the test."

"And you locked him in the bathroom."

"Yeah. That was easy enough to do. Of course, when I

did it, I had no idea that the fire-control bots were going to seal the room and cut off the oxygen supply. And when they did, I assumed that my father would be safe enough, fast asleep in the bathroom. They were only supposed to cut off the oxygen supply to the main room."

"You used an unlicensed comms unit? You have one on the ship?"

Laresta shrugged. "Doesn't everyone?"

Jonathan frowned. "I'm sure Shawn and the security bot are going to have a lot of questions for you," he said.

"I'll answer them. I was just trying to protect Ava, the same way she's trying to protect me."

Jonathan used his wrist unit to request the security team. They arrived very quickly and escorted Laresta away.

"You didn't say anything about her father dying well before the fire-control bots shut down the oxygen supply to the room," I said.

"I didn't want her to know that we knew that little detail, not yet. I want her to confess to everything else, to drugging the man, to locking him in the bathroom, to leaving him there to die. Only then will that little point become an issue."

"She killed her own father."

"He lied to her for much of her life."

"According to Ava, anyway."

"There is that. It's possible that Ava was lying. I suspect the truth is somewhere between the two stories, really. It generally is."

We walked back into the corridor together.

"What are you going to do now?" I asked him.

"I need to talk to the security bots about everything that Ava and Laresta told us. And I need to make sure that

Shawn doesn't mess everything up by saying something he shouldn't."

I nodded. "Good luck."

He walked me back to my cabin before continuing on down the corridor. I let myself in and grabbed Singer.

"We found the killer," I told her. "It was all very sad and a bit strange and a bunch of other things. I don't know what to think."

"Merroowwww," Singer said.

"Yeah, probably that."

I WAS HALFWAY through breakfast the next morning when a crew member walked into the room.

"Just stay where you are," he said with a sigh. "We're testing the system again."

Everyone in the room turned to watch as the man pulled a very long match out of his pocket. He lit it and held up his arm.

"Fire! Fire! Fire!" The fire-control bot flew into the room and did a full circuit of the space while the match continued to burn.

"Fire!" it said again, stopping over my table.

"There isn't anything on fire here," I said, quickly picking up my plate.

As the bot moved away, I shoveled my last few bites into my mouth. The bot hovered over the next table.

"Fire?" it said questioningly.

"My fingers are getting hot," the crew member complained, switching the match to his other hand.

"Fire," another bot said as it flew into the room.

It quickly joined the other bot where it was hovering over another table.

"Fire," the first bot said.

"Fire," the second agreed.

"Not here," the man at the table said anxiously. He picked up his coffee and downed it in a single swallow.

"It's here," the crew member shouted. "Over here."

The bots both clicked and whirred before one flew to the opposite side of the room.

"Fire detection mode on," it said. Lights began to flash on top of the bot. It moved forward in millinches, seemingly scanning for heat or flames.

"It's here," the crew member shouted again. "But it won't be in a minute. The match is about to burn out."

The second bot flew up to the ceiling and then began to scan from there. I could see the wide-beam scanner as it swept the room. For some reason, it kept stopping just short of the crew member at the room's center.

"Okay, let's just say this is a failed test," the crew member said. He waved his arm and extinguished the match.

"Fire!" the bot near the ceiling said.

It flew directly at the man, aiming a spray of water at him as it went. The man turned and ran away, right into the path of the second bot. That one began to spray foam at the man. Everyone in the dining room started to laugh as the man ran in circles, being sprayed continually by both bots.

"We're all going to die if there's ever a real fire," someone said. "But at least we've had some entertainment today."

The crew member finally ran out the door with both bots in pursuit. For a moment, no one moved. Then everyone simply resumed eating as if nothing had happened. A cleaning bot rolled out of the kitchen and began to soak up the water and foam that covered the floor, several tables, and a handful of passengers.

"I hope that was all of our excitement for today," I muttered as I got up to leave the room.

"Try not to find any bodies later, okay?" someone shouted at me as I headed for the door.

"I'll do my best," I replied flatly.

A few people laughed. I sighed.

"Twenty more sectors," I told myself as I walked back to my cabin. "Only twenty more sectors."

GAMBLING IN GALAXY SECTOR

A LADY ELIZABETH COZY IN SPACE

Release date: April 17, 2026

I'd known that Danveria was going to be different to anything I'd ever experienced before, even before I got on the shuttle to the planet famous for its casinos.

We were only a few days into Galaxy Sector and while gambling wasn't something I was interested in doing, I was eager to get off the *Lady Elizabeth* for a short while. The longer I spent on the luxury spaceship, the more I appreciated our occasional planetary excursions.

Considering how my life has been going since I left Cenclare, I shouldn't have been surprised when a case of mistaken identity got me dragged into an incredibly high-stakes game of poker. And I should have been even less shocked when one of the other players was murdered in the middle of the game.

ALSO BY DIANA XARISSA

The Lady Elizabeth Cozies in Space

Alibis in Alpha Sector

Bodies in Beta Sector

Corpses in Chaos Sector

Danger in Delta Sector

Enemies in Energy Sector

Fires in Flux Sector

Gambling in Galaxy Sector

The Midlife Crisis Mysteries

Anxious in Nevada

Bewildered in Florida

Confused in Pennsylvania

Dazed in Colorado

Exhausted in Ohio

Frustrated in Massachusetts

The Isle of Man Cozy Mysteries

Aunt Bessie Assumes

Aunt Bessie Believes

Aunt Bessie Considers

Aunt Bessie Decides

Aunt Bessie Enjoys

Aunt Bessie Finds

Aunt Bessie Goes

Aunt Bessie's Holiday

Aunt Bessie Invites

Aunt Bessie Joins

Aunt Bessie Knows

Aunt Bessie Likes

Aunt Bessie Meets

Aunt Bessie Needs

Aunt Bessie Observes

Aunt Bessie Provides

Aunt Bessie Questions

Aunt Bessie Remembers

Aunt Bessie Solves

Aunt Bessie Tries

Aunt Bessie Understands

Aunt Bessie Volunteers

Aunt Bessie Wonders

Aunt Bessie's X-Ray

Aunt Bessie Yearns

Aunt Bessie Zeroes In

The Aunt Bessie Cold Case Mysteries

The Adams File

The Bernhard File

The Carter File

The Durand File

The Evans File

The Flowers File

The Goodman File

The Howard File

The Irving File

The Jordan File

The Keller File

The Lawrence File

The Moss File

The Newton File

The Olson File

The Phelps File

The Quinn File

The Markham Sisters Cozy Mystery Novellas

The Appleton Case

The Bennett Case

The Chalmers Case

The Donaldson Case

The Ellsworth Case

The Fenton Case

The Green Case

The Hampton Case

The Irwin Case

The Jackson Case

The Kingston Case

The Lawley Case

The Moody Case

The Norman Case

The Osborne Case

The Patrone Case

The Quinton Case

The Rhodes Case

The Somerset Case

The Tanner Case

The Underwood Case

The Vernon Case

The Walters Case

The Xanders Case

The Young Case

The Zachery Case

The Janet Markham Bennett Cozy Thrillers

The Armstrong Assignment

The Blake Assignment

The Carlson Assignment

The Doyle Assignment

The Everest Assignment

The Farnsley Assignment

The George Assignment

The Hamilton Assignment

The Ingram Assignment

The Jacobs Assignment

The Knox Assignment

The Lock Assignment

The Miles Assignment

The Nichols Assignment

The Owens Assignment

The Palmer Assignment

The Quayle Assignment

The Isle of Man Ghostly Cozy Mysteries

Arrivals and Arrests

Boats and Bad Guys

Cars and Cold Cases

Dogs and Danger

Encounters and Enemies

Friends and Frauds

Guests and Guilt

Hop-tu-Naa and Homicide

Invitations and Investigations

Joy and Jealousy

Kittens and Killers

Letters and Lawsuits

Marsupials and Murder

Neighbors and Nightmares

Orchestras and Obsessions

Proposals and Poison

Questions and Quarrels

Roses and Revenge

Secrets and Suspects

Theaters and Threats

Umbrellas and Undertakers

Visitors and Victims

Weddings and Witnesses

Xylophones and X-Rays

Yachts and Yelps

Zephyrs and Zombies

The Margaret and Mona Ghostly Cozies

Murder at Atkins Farm

Murder at Barker Stadium

Murder at Collins Airfield

Murder at Dreeym Gorrym Point

Murder at Edgewater Lane

The Sunset Lodge Mysteries

The Body in the Annex

The Body in the Boathouse

The Body in the Cottage

The Body in the Dunk Tank

The Body in the Elevator

The Body in the Fountain

The Body in the Greenhouse

The Body in the Hallway

The Body in the Igloo

The Isle of Man Romances

Island Escape

Island Inheritance

Island Heritage

Island Christmas

The Later in Life Love Stories

Second Chances

Second Act

Second Thoughts

Second Degree

Second Best

Second Nature

Second Place

Second Dance

BOOKPLATES ARE NOW AVAILABLE

Would you like a signed bookplate for this book?

I now have bookplates (stickers) that I can personalize, sign, and send to you. It's the next best thing to getting a signed copy!

Send an email to diana@dianaxarissa.com with your mailing address (I promise not to use it for anything else, ever) and how you'd like your bookplate personalized and I'll sign one and send it to you.

There is no charge for a bookplate, but there is a limit of one per person.

ABOUT THE AUTHOR

Diana has been self-publishing since 2013, and she feels surprised and delighted to have found readers who enjoy the stories and characters that she imagines. Always an avid reader, she still loves nothing more than getting lost in fictional worlds, her own or others!

After being raised in Erie, Pennsylvania, and studying history at Allegheny College in Meadville, Pennsylvania, Diana pursued a career in college administration. She was living and working in Washington, DC, when she met her future husband, an Englishman who was visiting the city.

Following her marriage, Diana moved to Derbyshire. A short while later, she and her husband relocated to the Isle of Man. After ten years on the island, during which Diana earned a Master's degree in the island's history, they made the decision to relocate again, this time to the US.

Now living near Buffalo, New York, Diana and her husband live with their daughter, a student at the University at Buffalo. Their son is now living and working just outside of Boston, Massachusetts, giving Diana an excuse to travel now and again.

Diana also writes mystery/thrillers set in the not-too-distant future as Diana X. Dunn and Young Adult fiction as D.X. Dunn.

She is always happy to hear from readers. You can write to her at:

Diana Xarissa Dunn
PO Box 72
Clarence, NY 14031.

Find Diana at: DianaXarissa.com
E-mail: Diana@dianaxarissa.com

Made in United States
Cleveland, OH
08 May 2025

16770071R00118